Memoirs of the dead
Presented by Your daily dose of fear

Memoirs of the dead
Presented by your daily dose of fear
By
Aaron Shupert
ILLUSTRATIONS BY
Faith Oswald
FaithnOswald@gmail.com

To my love, Samantha,
My wonderful mother,
and all the Yddof fans

Thank you for making this possible

-PREFACE-

This book took a few months to write, and I could not be happier with the way it turned out. When I first began writing the stories, I really didn't have any kind of direction. I was kind of flying blindly. A title was suggested to me. That title was memoirs of the end. While writing the title final title sort of popped out of my brain by accident while trying to type the suggestion, which was at that time the working title. When I read the words 'Memoirs of the dead' on the computer screen, I got excited, and knew I had something special! As the stories flowed onto the page the books title became more and more perfect.

This book came about from all the support and love that I received from fans and followers, they are the reason that I am driven to make my own horror instead of just being content to watch, and read others.

I'm Wickid, and this is your daily dose of fear.

-INTRODUCTION-

Death, what exactly do we know about it? Well not a lot to be honest, there is no solid way to communicate with the other side. As a matter of fact we still argue about whether there is actually an other side. Some people claim that there is a heaven and Hell, while others claim that the dead are reincarnated over and over until they can reach nirvana. Other people still believe that there is nothing. We get one time around this life and that's it. There are people who believe everything in between. Who's correct? Are any of them correct? Who's wrong? And are any of them wrong?

Death isn't always necessarily the end. The dead come back as ghosts, or angels and demons. Sometimes the dead just don't stay dead, their lifeless bodies get up and shamble around. Some just don't die, for whatever reason there are some people that death just doesn't come for. Some fear death, some embrace it. Some are fascinated and some remain blissfully ignorant. Which one are you?

If you're not the latter continue reading. In this book, you can read several accounts of when the reaper comes. Several *final moments* this is a recollection of their stories.

These are the memoirs of the dead.

-THE SKY WAS ANGRY-

It started about a month ago. It was a warm summer Saturday morning when the rays of the sun shone through my window, and bathed me in it's light. I stirred and my eyes slowly opened. It was like I was in my own special movie. I was on break and had nothing to do today, my plans? Sit around the house, eat junk food, and play my Xbox. I was thinking about binging a new TV show that started streaming today. I laid in my bed for about twenty minutes before getting up using sheer will power. My legs were a little shaky as they seemed to have not been on the same page as me about getting up. I toppled to the floor. Pretty hard. "Honey are you alright?" My mom was a sweet woman.

"Yeah mom my shirt hit the floor."

"It sounded a lot heavier than a shirt." Her tone was flat, and unamused she knew what was coming next but she still set me up.

"I was still wearing it." I laughed.

"Hardy harr." She called out to me. "Get to the dining room, I'm actually just making breakfast." She stopped for a second, "And try not to fall down the stairs on your way here." This time she laughed, and it was my turn to be unamused. I did what she asked though and I got breakfast. She grabbed her stuff for work, then she came in close to me, she beckoned me with her finger and I leaned in. she looked around as to see if anyone was watching, or listening, than leaned in to me. I thought she was going to tell me a secret. She grabbed me and kissed my forehead. I pulled back making disapproving noises, and wiping my forehead. She had a big smile on her face and then began laughing. As if she pulled off the greatest trick ever.

"Get moving." I urged. "You're going to be late for work, and I'm going to be late for all the nothing I have planned." She nodded and agreed.

"I love you sweetie, try not to have too much fun." I groaned back at her and impatiently waited for her to leave. She did, and I headed back to my room and powered on my Xbox it was time for some games! Hours were wasted playing call of duty, I had all the skins, all the unlockables, I could even do some sweet trick shots. After a while though, it was becoming boring, my mom was always getting on my case about getting outside and enjoying the sun. I felt a little guilty, like, I know I should but then again I'm lazy and don't want to. I continued to play until the monotony of the game got to be too much. My mom would be home any minute and I haven't done anything all day, not hadn't even cleaned up after myself and the mess I made. I turned the console off, walked downstairs, cleaned up the kitchen and headed out the front door.

I was on the way to see my best friend, we were gonna get some pizza for dinner, and then go back to his house, and play cod. I gave my mother a call and let her know that I would be staying at Tony's place for the night, the two of us were going to see a movie the next day. She didn't have a problem with it. That night tony and I stayed up way too late. I was getting too tired to keep playing games, my reflexes had slowed tremendously, so we put those down, and threw on some TV. It was about two in the morning when I had a brilliant idea... well it was brilliant at the time at least. "hey tony, I got a little something to make this night more interesting." I told him. I grabbed my backpack and reached. I produced two energy drinks

"You know me so well." He said smiling. I nodded, as I pulled two more out of my bag. He looked approvingly at them, I handed them to him, and pulled out yet another two. I should mention these are not the little cans, but in reality I had six of the giant energy drinks.

"Lets each chug these cans and then tell some horror stories. Well I got through two of my cans and my mind was racing, I was shaking and felt like I needed to run around in circles, tony seemed to be having a similar reaction. Our solution? Lets go walking around the middle of the night. We both got on our phones and began swapping our favorite scary stories The small little suburb we lived in was so creepy at night. Nothing but the street lights casting illumination onto us, the moon was not in the sky tonight, and the stars seemed just a bit brighter for it. We walked around for a while, for as long as we could. The combination of lack of sleep, energy drinks,and ghost stories, had us imagining some crazy crap. We went back to his place and crashed hard.

When I awoke, Tony was already up, it was weird, he was just standing at the window staring out it. "Hey uhh, Tony? Are you ok man?" I asked him, he didn't respond, he didn't even move. I shifted in my spot. He was making me uncomfortable. "Hey tony." I called a little louder.

"Come take a look at this." He called back, he paused and then motioned for me to come over. I reluctantly stood up and walked over to him

"Man you're kind of scaring me man, what are you..." my voice trailed off before I could finish the question, I stood there slack jaw as I stared. The sky was dark. The thickest clouds I've seen in my life. Almost no light was penetrating. I felt uneasy. I felt more than uneasy I felt afraid. After standing there for a minute I started to speak. "Were we supposed to get clouds today?"

"No." We just stood there in silence for a minute

"Well, maybe we should check the news." I grabbed my phone, before I could get my internet open, it started blasting a rock song, any other day, I would have enjoyed it but today, with the sky looking like it did, with the fear, and unease that I felt, I was in no mood to rock out. It was mom calling, I don't think I've ever been so relieved. "H-hello?" I stammered a little bit.

"Oh sweetie, thank god, I'm on my way home from work, please get home, I'll see you soon."

"Mom... what's going on?"

I sat there waiting for her to explain it. "I don't know." I could hear the fear in her voice. We hung up and tony looked at me waiting for an answer, I shrugged, and looked back at my phone. After a few minutes of searching we found no legitimate answers. Just crazy ramblings about the end times, and the government. I put the phone in my pocket and walked back to the window. Tony followed suit. We stood there for another few minutes before we heard commotion in the front room. It was Tony's parents. They made sure we were ok.

"I need to get home." I informed them. Tony's dad, Chris, gave me a flashlight. The clouds were getting thicker. The sky, darker. I happily took the flashlight, "I'll get this back to you asap." I promised, grabbing my backpack. Then headed for the door.

"Please call tony when you get home," his mother pleaded. "I know that it's just a couple blocks, but with this strange weather..."

"I will." I stopped her mid sentence to reassure her. I opened the door, and immediately realized how cold it was. Colder than last night had been, much colder. It was cold enough that I was shivering, wanting a coat. Yesterday it was sunny, and bright in the eighties, and today, I needed a jacket and a flashlight.

I got home shortly before my mom, when she arrived I was just standing in the lawn looking at the clouds that have nearly blocked out the light entirely. I shone my flashlight through the darkness, it illuminated a path quite effectively, I'm sure they must have paid a good amount for this flashlight. When she got out of her car she came running up to me and embraced me in a big hug, I swear she was trying to squeeze the life out of me. I groaned and she let me go. "Mom, have you heard anything about this? Do you know what's going on?" I questioned her, she was quiet for a minute.

"I'm sorry honey, I don't know anything solid, just the wild rumors." I nodded in agreement. "Come on inside, let me make you some dinner." I followed her into the house, through the living room I was surprised when I caught a glimpse of the clock. It was around two forty five. I looked back at the window it was dark enough to be midnight out there. Thinking about it all, a chill slowly crawled it's way down my spine and I shivered.

My mom made chili dogs and macaroni, she knew it was my favorite meal. I knew she made it to help try to calm my nerves. And to be honest it really did work. I ate dinner and I felt better. Mom asked me if I'd watch a movie with her, I wanted to, but I didn't want to admit that I was scared. So I groaned with disapproval in response. "Please honey, with the sky doing what it's doing I just want you with me, it would make me feel better if you could stay with me and watch a movie. I'd feel safe, protected." My mom was a liar. I knew that she knew that I was scared and in reality did just want my mommy. But I was sixteen, there is no way I could admit that. My teenage ego would never allow it. I smiled at her, with love and appreciation, she patted the couch cushion next to her, I sat down and she wrapped her arms around me, squeezed me, then started our favorite movie to watch together. Toy story.

We got a little ways into the movie, and I was feeling good, just a few minutes after three thirty though, it all changed. It felt like an earthquake. But it was the sky, I don't know how to describe it really. The sky was angry, it sounded like the sky was being ripped open, the thunder roared shaking everything. Dishes, and nick knacks and most other things not nailed down fell off shelves and crashed to the floor. Car alarms started screaming in the distance trying their best to be heard over the thunder. It was deafening. At the same time the sky was set ablaze. First streaks of light ripping through the clouds. Then the real bolts of lightning began. Each one lit up the sky, lit up everything. We had to cover our eyes, the light was blinding. The bolts hadn't been striking the ground though, they were shooting through the clouds. When it had settled down, I was didn't dare let myself feel relief. I held my breath for a long time. The sky opened up and started pouring rain down. I let out a deep sigh, everything would be ok soon, and I fell asleep.

When I awoke the rain was still coming down, I figured it must be late, the lights were out and it was pitch black out. I pulled myself off the couch, careful not to disturb my mom. I went to the closet and grabbed her a blanket, and draped it over her. I headed over to the window and looked out. The rain was coming down, really hard. The street was beginning to flood, the drain must have clogged. I stretched wide, it felt good, and started to make my way back toward the stairs to go to my bedroom. I lost my breath and could feel my legs trying to collapse under my body when I caught a glimpse of my clock. it was ten till five. I hurried back over to the window. The water was just over the curb. I rushed out into the lawn with my flashlight. It was flooded as far down as I could see, it wasn't just my block that was flooded. Even if all of our drains were clogged, how could we have that much water in an hour and a half? I ran back into the house, in just the few short minutes that I had been outside I was completely drenched. I convinced myself that everything was fine, it just happened to be raining quite hard, that's why it's so flooded. Headed upstairs into my room, changed into something dry that I could sleep in and crawled into bed.

I woke up to my mom on the phone, she sounded frantic and scared. I rushed down the stairs to see what was going on. She was on the phone, and she was visibly distressed. Barely noticed that I was in the room. I walked by her and turned on the TV, it just showed a black screen with a service unavailable message. I assumed that's what's got my mom all worked up, and I just read the signals wrong. I walked to the door, the clouds are still out and it's still pouring. The water level is up to our porch. If it doesn't stop raining soon it may flood the house. My mom got off the phone, and looked over at me, we just stood in silence for a few minutes before I finally spoke. "Mom?" I said inquisitively, "What's going on?"

"The rain, this storm, it's everywhere. So far the scientists have no idea what's causing it, where it came from, or how it came to be. They don't know how to stop it." I looked at her stunned. I didn't know what to say, I didn't know what was going to happen. I was terrified, she was terrified.

A month passed, and the down pour has only gotten heavier. power has been knocked out. It was gone in the first week, the clouds only grow thicker and darker as time goes by. By the second night the water had risen into our house, mom and I began sleeping up stairs while we waited for help. After three nights, no light came through from the sun at all. And then when the power went out hello almost total darkness. We were relying on crank flashlights and other such power generation devices. The only news and updates we could still get were through our phones. The government would send daily text messages to everyone, keeping us informed. About ten days after the storm started the water had forced us onto the roof. The house was completely flooded. That's when we were moved. They took us to really tall buildings in the city, it was crowded and uncomfortable but it had to do.

Shortly after we were moved the cell towers must have fallen because the signals on the cell phones went out. And the rain kept pouring. We still have no idea why. At twenty days the water reached halfway up the building, this was unreal, there's not this much water on earth. Or at least I had thought. But the rain continued to come down. It's rare but every so often a bolt of lighting will cut through the sky, and illuminate the world, for just a split second. Followed by earth shaking thunder. It's so terrifying.

When we hit twenty five days after the storm started, the water level seem to plateau, that is, it stopped rising. For a split second we cheered. Oh god we actually celebrated this new turn of events. In less than a month this, the flooding, the rain, the clouds the storm, this, became the new normal, and any little victory was cause for rejoice. And the flood not rising anymore well, that was great cause for rejoice. My god we were happy. We were happy and we partied all through the night and into the next day. It rained and we partied.

Our celebration was cut abruptly short, in a spectacular and terrifying manner. The lightning that usually flashed cloud to cloud. It struck. A bolt of the terrifying intense electricity fell from the heavens, and hit a building close to us. The power was too much for the building to handle And it began to crumble. The buildings directly around it shook so violently their glass shattered, I thought ours was going to. But thankfully, our building just shook. That first strike was four days ago. Now the lightning strikes a couple of times a day. I didn't know how long we we're going to survive the lightning. How long we we're going to survive the rain. At the month mark the lighting did stop only our building breaks the surface of the water anymore. A lone beacon in a brand new ocean. And at thirty five days it was apparent that the water level had begun rising again. It rose at a very slow pace, but it was rising. We've been totally cut off from the outside world. I mean, if there even is an outside world anymore, it's just water as far as the eye can see anymore. The chopper that used to bring people and supplies, it stopped showing up. I'm sure it got struck down. Luckily, if you can call it lucky, we have food for months, years even.

In the bible, in the days of Noah and his ark The rain lasted for forty days and forty nights. I can live with the darkness, I can live with the cold, I can live with the lightning. It's been forty five days.

I wish the rain would stop.

-GIRL WITH AN AX-

More fun

I'm so glad you're here I've been waiting for you
There's so many fun things for us to do
We can play with mommy but not with dad
When he finds us he's gonna be mad
We'll play with our dolls and drink fake tea
I'm so glad you came to play with me
I really don't have all that many friends
But now that you're here I'll never be lonely again
They keep me locked up and tell me I'm sick
They don't want me to be happy it's all a big trick
But now that you're here I just cannot be sad
Oh you're the best friend a person could have
The things you want me to do they seem kind of bad
You say you're my friend it's ok I can trust you
It's only a game and I wouldn't want to lose
But mommy doesn't like it when I talk to you
And I really don't think she likes what we do
Stop talking to yourself and get in your bed
Your friend is not real that's what mother said
Well mommy doesn't talk as much now that she's dead
But you're right she's more fun with an ax in her head

She'll never recover

"We found her in a basement; she must have been down there for a week. It's a goddamned miracle she survived; the baby didn't, starved to death. Right in her arms. She's never gonna recover. Imagine a four year old going through that. She was smart enough though really\ smart actually, hiding under a body like that. But to lie motionless for a week like that, covered in blood, holding her dead baby sister. She'll never recover."

"She witnessed it all, she had to have. Her entire family, those sick bastards! I don't know how she managed to not get caught. We've got her in a group home now, trying to get her into a nice new family, hopefully she'll forget. Such a tragedy though, the mental scarring will never heal, I'm sure of that. She may grow up, move on, and forget but... She'll never recover."

"She woke up screaming again last night, she wakes up screaming most nights. I think it's the nightmares. She's reliving that night, the night that her family was, was murdered. I'm worried about her; I don't know what to do. I've taken her to therapists and nothing seems to help, she's starting doing bad things, she set a fire. She, well, she said that someone told her to do it. I've become fearful of her, and I'm fearful that she'll never recover."

Man in the woods

The moon is barely poking through the treetops on the cloudless night as she walks through the woods, scared, cold and alone. She's dirty, and tired, she's been walking through the woods for hours and hours. Knees scraped from falling down and cuts on her hands and legs. She's on the verge of tears. A big man appears rather tall and on the huskier side. She notices his scruffy beard. The tattered clothes with dry brownish stains make her nervous, they look like blood stains. She's visibly scared of this man, but she doesn't move. She stands there shaking, attempting to hold back the crying.

"What are you doing out here so late young lady?" His voice, while rough, has a kindness to it and being a child of no more than eight or nine, a kind voice makes her forget her fears. She looks up at him and gives him a little smile through the tears that have begun welling in her eyes. "

I-I can't find my friend." She manages to choke out. "We came in here exploring so long ago, it was actually still daytime. My momma was gonna fix us some lunch soon, but we wanted to play for just a bit longer, and then she, she disappeared." At this point the small girl loses it and begins weeping.

"It's ok sweetie, let's get you back to my shack, we can get you warm, maybe get some food in your belly, then we can go out and look for your friend." The young girl happily agrees, while wiping away her tears, and with perfect timing her stomach begins grumbling the man flashes her an awkward smile while she's blushing. This made her uncomfortable again.

He leads her deeper into the woods until they reach a little one room shack. Many candles rest on homemade shelves and the whole thing seems like a cozy albeit small space. There's a fire pit out by the opening; although the fire wasn't going, she could feel the warmth of the coals as she walked by it. Above the pit there was some kind of meat suspended in one of those contraptions that reminds the girl of the way cartoons roast food. The meat that the man gives her is delicious but she cannot quite pinpoint the flavor, she does not recognize the type of meat that it is.

"Oh I'm sure that you've never had this type of meat." The man says to her, recognizing the confusion on her face. "They don't exactly sell this in supermarkets." His grinning made the girl even more uncomfortable.

"Why do you..." Her voice trails off as he glares at her, the grin still on his face.

"Why do I live in the woods?" The girl nods. "Well... let's just say, I enjoy my privacy. People would not be happy about the lifestyle that I enjoy or what I do." This was enough. Even a young girl knows when it becomes time to leave; she quickly stands up and thanks the man for the meal, but insists she really needs to find her friend. The man follows her out of the shack. "Don't worry sweetheart, we'll look together."

After a good amount of time looking she heard him call out to her saying that he found something she might want to see. The young girl hurries over to examine what he found, forgetting her discomfort. He stops her before she gets there. "I have some... unfortunate news." His voice was still rough, the kindness, along with the grin was gone. He turns around, and she follows him for a few steps, then stops. The man gestures at the ground. There lying dead, bloody, with her skull caved in, was the girl that she's been looking for.

"I have some unfortunate news as well." The girl's voice

was as cold, and as sharp as the ax that was buried into the back of the man's head. His eyes roll back as he falls onto the carcass of a black bear, one just like he had fed her earlier. "She wasn't my friend... She was just some bitch that told me my only real friend was imaginary, and that I was crazy. She kept saying that my friend wasn't real; this made my friend extremely angry. My friend was right though I can play with her now and she's much more fun. I'm sure you will be too now.

I know what you are

It was a quiet cool night and there was a lone little girl skipping down the street. Skipping and whistling. I'll tell you what it was creepy as hell just like something out of a horror movie, but I was being ridiculous right? It's just a night owl, a kid who just couldn't sleep, she probably lived close by and went out for some fresh air. That and possibly some bad parenting for letting her be out so late. I sat watching her from my second story window, I studied her, disgusted that parents could leave a girl so young alone, and I thought maybe a lesson is in order. Strange though almost as if on command she stopped. She stopped skipping, her happy whistle was gone, she just kind of froze in place. This is my chance I thought, I started to pull away when she moved again, only this time towards my house. How did I get so lucky?!

I was on my way downstairs when the bell rang, I live alone so I called out "I'll be right there" I finished down the steps and was at the door. 'Was I going to do this again?' The thought pushed it's way into my head 'I haven't in so long, I don't need this anymore. I've gotten better.' My urges were suppressed the thoughts I had managed to control; I cracked the door and peeked out, the girl, beautiful, lovely, and smiling a warm innocent smile. I looked around I had to double check she was alone, she was. At that point I opened the door wide, and invited her in. Turning to lead the way I took a step forward seen a bright flash of lights then everything was black.

I thought I was dead I woke up in my basement, in my play room, weird I don't remember coming down here, then I seen the little girl slumped over in a chair, my chair. It dawned on me when I went to move that, I'm strapped down, how did I get here. I pulled at the restraints, I was in here good. My struggling alerted her, she stirred, slowly rising to her feet, I struggled harder. Damn I made those restraints good, she stood looking at me right in the face. My restraints were made child height so I had to kneel. She stared at me, looking into my soul that same smile on her face, even in this position it was still warm and friendly. She reached behind the chair she had once rested on, and produced an ax; the handle was about as tall as her. From the looks of it she'd never be able to use it.

"I know what you are." She said to me, "And I know what you do." I laughed nervously and attempted to squeak out a response, but was cut off "I wonder, do you know who I am? Do you know what I do?" I shook my head, "You'd like to know wouldn't you, you'd like that satisfaction?" She got a grip on the ax, her eyes and smile, unchanged but somehow went cold. "I'm just a little girl." And with that the ax swung up, and then down. Fire radiated from the top of my head and everything went black. I think I'm dead.

-CHESS WITH DEATH-

I had always heard that when it was your time, when death came for you, if you could beat him in a game he wouldn't take you. If you managed to best him then he would let you live. I like many people I never gave this too much thought though, I was sure it was just another legend. It was a way to give hope to the hopeless. A way to allow people who are at the end of their life to have some dignity. I figured that it would allow people to feel like they have a choice, allow them to not be powerless in the face of death. But ultimately a bunch of hokey.

I knew that this wasn't true, once your time comes, it's over. There's no angel of death that comes and takes you away. There's no being or entity that meets you, and plays a game with your life in the balance. That being said, there was always something in the back of my brain. Something that compelled me to take up chess. I was good at it, no it was more than that. I was amazing, as a child I was considered a prodigy.

As I grew, my skill did as well. I took on people much older than myself and I won. After over coming local champions, I rose through the ranks. I didn't play for fame, or fortune. I played for fun, at least that's what I told myself. Honestly though, I'm not sure why I was so drawn to the game. I don't really think that death was on my mind as a small child. Regardless of the reasoning though, I honed my skills. Chess became my life. I beat the best players in the world, and at the age of sixteen, I became a grandmaster. Sure I didn't become the youngest gm in history, but it was still a pretty great accomplishment.

I didn't really have much of a life in high school, I did the home school thing, while I trained to become the gm, and then my life turned all to chess, by the time I was thirty four, there were whispers of me being considered a god. This is a term given to players to seem to always play a perfect game of chess. I never thought of myself like that, as a god. I never seen myself as playing perfectly. I always felt like I could improve, there was always room for me to get better, I continued to push myself. A woman soon entered my life, and she was the most beautiful woman I had ever seen. She was kind, and sweet, her voice was like an angel singing praises to god. I needed to get to know her, and I did.

I grew close to her, I treated her like the queen she was and in turn she showered me with devotion, loyalty affection, and genuine love. We were happy together, and I stepped away from chess. I had known she was the one since the first time I met her at a chess championship. Once I had worked up the nerve, I proposed, she said yes with overwhelming excitement. The engagement didn't last long, just long enough for the wedding to be planned, and we were married. Together we had three children, my amazing wife had given me three wonderful daughters. They were as beautiful as their mother and as smart as their father. They would grow up to be deadly! My life was more perfect than any one person deserves. More perfect that I could have dreamed of in my wildest imagination. But it was getting ready to fall apart.

As I said I had stepped away from chess, my family demanded my attention and I was more than pleased to give it all to them, they were my reason for living. The reason that I woke up in the mornings. They were the reason that I settled down in a nice quiet job. While playing chess was fun, and it did make me money, I didn't feel the money was sustainable. The cash flow wasn't reliable, and consistent. It didn't allow me to plan for retirement, and it didn't offer benefit's to my family. So I found a little job in a local office, just a desk job, nothing special, certainly not as glamorous as a chess grand master, but it paid the bills, and it was good for my family.

This was all I needed in life. Until the day that my past came back to haunt me in the form of an old rival of mine. He had tracked me down, found my phone number and given me a call. I wish I hadn't answered that call. I wish I hadn't agreed to meet, I wish I hadn't accepted his challenge of a *friendly* game of chess. He told me that he had heard I fell off, quit playing, that I was a washed up has been. Well I was, but my pride would not allow me to admit that, and let it go. So I agreed.

When I moved that first pawn, the past came flooding back to me like a tsunami washing away a town, or an army of pieces under my control advancing towards a defenseless king. We played. It was an amazing match. The pieces flew, I couldn't believe how good he had gotten. He was right on par with me and the battle was intense. I'm not sure when it happened but all the sudden, I was losing ground, he was taking my pieces and I couldn't seem to stop him. I had a brilliant move in my head, I made it. I had him. It's over I leaned back, and grinned smugly there's nothing he could do, I would win with my next move and we both knew it. "Checkmate." The word echoed through the coffee shop. It echoed through my head. I looked at the board confused, unable to comprehend what he had just said to me. My mouth was dry, and I could barely find words.

What?" I choked out eyes still fixed on the board, staring unwavering.

"Check," he paused, I could feel his gaze, I could feel

him wanting to gloat, "mate." I continued to stare. He was right! I made a dumb mistake. I missed such an obvious play. Me. The person who was once referred to as a god, made a misplay that anyone with basic knowledge of the game, wouldn't have made. My world began to crumble, how could I have been beaten, how could I have made such an amateur mistake? I began my downward spiral. All of the sudden, I felt as if I needed to begin playing again. At first it was here and there, I had an application on my phone, and I set that to the hardest difficulty, but it was as simple as beating a child. it was not made for someone of my skill, I believe the app was made to introduce people to chess, I found a computer program that was much better, it challenged me, it learned from my play styles. It forced me to always look for new options because it would counter my previously used strategies. I began playing whenever I had a bit of free time. When my family were in bed, on my lunch hour. I felt myself becoming a man obsessed but I couldn't help it.

Soon enough playing in my free time was no longer sufficient however, the addiction, the obsession, it spilled over into my personal and professional lives, and they both suffered for it. I began first playing at work, instead of doing my job, and I got away with it for a while, until my work became so backed up that the boss began to notice, I was reprimanded, but given the opportunity to catch up on my work, I did, but it didn't take long for chess to take the front seat again. My work became backed up once again, and I was fired.

Slowly my home life deteriorated as well, when I lost my job my wife began to work to take care of the family and give me a little bit of time off. This only made things worse, as it gave me more time to lose myself. When the time came for me to find a new job, I didn't, I became more withdrawn from my family, barely spending anytime with them at all. I conquered the computer program, I could beat it in my sleep. I set my sights on human opponents again, and I began traveling trying to find and play the best. And I did play the best, and beat the best. Over the next five or six years, I slowly regained my spot at the top. I went back home after a particularly long trip and found the house empty. My wife, had had enough of me. she had enough of being put after the game, of me putting the game before the kids, before everything else. I couldn't blame her.

I wished my wife well, and sent her signed papers for a divorce, and custody of the children. Along with said papers I sent a note giving her possession of the house, bank accounts, and most other valuable things. I once again felt a passion for chess, and a burning need to be the best at it. To be unbeatable. I worked everyday until I earned the title of god once again. I was back at the top, and I planned on staying here this time. Nothing was going to derail me. I devoted my entire life to the game.

As I grew older, as my time on this planet grew shorter, and as I grew wiser and closer to the end. I knew, and was able to accept that I had not played for love, or passion, but for fear, and determination. I was going to die, that much I knew. But when I met the reaper, the angel of death. I would not be going with him. I had not been playing chess, you see, I had in fact been training for the ultimate contest of life and death and when I beat the reaper, I would be allowed to stay! Now accepting the end goal I continued to do what I could to hone my skills. But there were none who could provide a significant challenge and I grew bored. That was until I came across a computer called emerald green. This was said to be a spiritual successor to deep blue a computer that in the nineties beat the world champion. This computer beat me, pretty bad. At first that is. But slowly over the time span of a few years and hundreds of matches. I slowly began to stalemate it. then by some miracle, I was able to overcome it. I began to outplay the best chess player be it human or machine. I was at the end of my life. And I was ready.

It was a bad heart that seemed would ultimately take me. it began deteriorating slowly, and I was in and out of the hospital. Then my first attack hit. It had been around. Twenty-one years since I met my wife and ultimately gave up chess. It had been about fifteen since I lost her. The heart attack put me down, and I was in the hospital for quite a while. I wasn't scared of death, albeit a young one, I had only reached fifty-five, but I welcomed it because I knew that I would be able to beat him. The worst part of this time was the loneliness. I almost died from the heart attack, and yet no one came to see me. I didn't see my ex wife, I didn't even see my kids, I cried for a good long time and vowed that no matter what I would have a relationship with my children when I came back. My wife, she had probably moved on, I hoped for at least a friendship with her.

Sometime later, within the year, while I slept, the big one came. My heart stopped beating suddenly and I couldn't make it to a phone to get an ambulance. I knew this was the end. I knew this was the beginning. I waited for death. I had given up a lifetime to train and I knew that I would be able to defeat him in a game of chess. I knew that I possess the skills to triumph. I knew that the reaper was no match for me. I knew these things in my heart I knew them to be true. I was wrong.

I was not wrong about my skills. I was the best chess player there ever was. No one could beat me. The problem? When I died. When the heart attack took me. when I stepped into the void where I would finally meet my greatest opponent.

He wasn't there.

-GOD IS DEAD-

Religion was dying. For far too long religion, and the religious leaders had brought about wars, hate and discrimination. Religious folk stood in the way of progress, they tried and in a lot of cases were successful in stripping away people's civil rights. There was no common human decency for the people that lived life in any manner of way that they disagreed with. Religion stood in the way of science and knowledge slowing and even halting man's ability to make advances. Millions of lives had been lost in holy wars, waged based on what was supposed to be a merciful all loving god, through the refusal of modern medicine, and senseless murder because their loving god didn't approve of what the victim was doing. What kind of loving god would ever allow this to take place?

Millions of lives lost through famine, drought, earthquakes, wildfires, tornadoes, floods and all other manner of natural disaster. Lives lost or ruined by abusive parents, sexual slavery, and every type of cruelty that one can imagine. These people should have had special places in the deepest darkest pit's of Hell reserved for them, for what they've done. But the church would always teach that even the worst offenders could be let into heaven, simply by repenting on their death bed. That no matter what someone did, no matter how horrible they were in life, there was no consequence because by repenting they could still enter the kingdom of heaven. What kind of god would allow this? Would allow that kind of evil into paradise.

Religion has stood in the way of human evolution our brains got bigger and bigger, and as a whole humanity got smarter and smarter. But as a species humanity has been continuously held back. Religion had retarded the progress of science. They shamed, ostracized and attacked free thinkers. The fear that they may finally have some kind of proof that disagrees with their god would cause them to lash out, ignoring facts, and attempting to quell any thoughts on the mater. Attempting to shutdown anyone and any research they were doing that touched on anything that questioned blind faith. Religion has almost been the end of humanity. People that follow religion had spread hate and ignorance, while claiming to love. They would destroy, and take, they would kill, and judge, and all while claiming mercy and grace. They hypocrisy was staggering.

But as it always does, the world just kept turning and time kept flowing forward. Nothing could stop that. People grew old and people died. As they did a new generation would take their place. And as this new generation grew up, change was in the air. A mirror held up to the religious people, they were able to see their hypocrisy. Put on display were all the tragedies caused by religion. And the world was shown what evils rose out of it, disguised in love. Slowly the older society eventually died out, and the new generation, having grown up seeing the consequences of blind faith, began to abandon religion all together. They grew up seeing the toxicity of it all, the pain it caused, the lives that it cost.

It took decades and decades but one by one religions began falling. It started with the most wild cults. Even as the most outlandish examples fell the big religions already had rumblings. The denominations of the big ones began to crumble, until the world was left with Islam, Buddhism, Hinduism, and Christianity. They hung on the longest, but eventually even these religions completely died as all but the hardcore believers abandoned their faith and turned away from their respective gods.

Across the world the churches were just outright

abandoned at first as the congregations slowly disbanded, without offerings, churches had no way to sustain and with governments overturning the separation of church and state, they became required to pay taxes. Over time the abandoned former places of worship were converted things that humanity actually needed. Things like homeless shelters, soup kitchens, and other such buildings to help the less fortunate.

The homeless were clothed and fed, trained and put to work. In the wake of the church crumbling homelessness came to an end, first in the first world, and then over the globe. It became a societal normality to spend Sunday with family and friends, relaxing and enjoying each others company. This led to the families being closer, which in turn lowered things like drug addiction, suicide, and other such problems like alcoholism. The money that was going to churches was turned back into the economy which boosted it. With a boosted economy, more jobs were created enough for everyone. No one had to live in poverty anymore. Crime almost completely disappeared. Wars began to end. Without religion, and the prejudice, and judgment that would come along with that, to divide the world fighting between the countries began to die down. And eventually they began to work together and slowly worked toward a one world government. Under the one world first, second, and third worlds did not exist, all countries were equal with the same laws and punishments, as well as, help financially, and in any other fashion for those in need.

Disease after disease fell as medicine became extremely advanced. Without the hopelessness of prayer medicine was invested in. Death was a disease that was eliminated, and life was great. No one ha to grow old, and no one had to experience the crushing loss of death.

Overcrowding would have been an issue if not for the ingenuity and drive towards science that was collectively had without religion. Humanity began to pour themselves out into the dark void of space. Exploring, mining and ultimately colonizing the other rocky planets in our solar system, and neighboring systems. God had fallen out of the public eye completely, and became the stuff of old legends. Talked about in a romantic nature, and thought of fondly as a figure that the ignorant people of the past had worshiped, with the greatest of intentions. He was taught in schools as a warning of what can happen people follow blindly on the basis of faith without question. Religion was dead. God was dead. He joined the ranks of other ancient and almost forgotten deities such as Zeus, and Cronos. Without god, without religion, cults were non existent, ritualistic killings, and suicides, all became things of a darker, more barbaric time. Earth had become a peaceful place, a paradise even. All people lived in harmony, in equality. the world had never known such acceptance, and love.

He walked the earth to and fro, he looked over and watched everything that had happened. He watched the transformation, gleeful and happy. He truly admired his work. He was proud of the things he had done. He had performed miracles. Guided the human race to perfection. He was overjoyed, the job was done effectively, and completely. Peace, love, and harmony now reigned across the land, and across the solar system. Humanity had become what he had always known that it could become. They were more beautiful than he could ever imagine. Humanity as a whole was happy.

Satisfied with his journey, satisfied with the work he'd done, and satisfied with the wondrous outcome. He returned home. He sat on his glorious throne, a place that he had not been in a thousand years as he worked to shape humanity into the beauty that it should have been all along. Being away from his home for such a long time will now finally be worth it, all the time and effort he spent helping humanity grow, he could now enjoy watching the outcome of everything that he had done. A wicked smile slowly crept across his face. Surrounded by suffering and pain, torturous screams echoing throughout. He was overwhelmed with pride, his plan had succeeded. In giving humanity all it's ever wanted, in ending the wars the turmoil, the pain, and the suffering. He won.

"Father, it's over, humanity has turned their back on us." He spoke with an incredible sadness in his voice. His father sat silently, but the look of defeat was written clearly across his face. His son could read it plainly. He knew what was going to have to happen, he knew what his father was going to do. He understood that it was the only way but that didn't make it hurt any less. His heart ached. He knew that his father would have to break the promise he had made thousands of years before...

Jesus wept.

-ALIEN WORLD-

We were on the lookout for any intelligent life that we could find. We scanned the heavens looking for any signs of it, or any planets that may be suitable to contain life. Our sciences had advanced in ways our ancestors could not even have dreamed. We had technology that even a few generations ago would have seemed impossible, even theoretically and we were still a smart people then advancing at light speed. Even so they wouldn't be able to comprehend what we have now. The ships, the computers, the brilliant minds that we produce. It's nothing short of incredible.

We finally found a blue rock in a distant solar system. We studied it heavily as it seemed to have all the makings of a planet that could indeed host life. That being the case it didn't seem to have any notable life that held higher intelligence, that is, we couldn't seem to find any on our scanners. we decided that while there was no observable life, it had huge oceans which may be hiding life under the surface. If there was no life to be found, we could use what natural resources the planet has and mine them for our planet. As we approached we could see the planet had huge areas of land, but they were brown. It was full of deserts, it seemed uninhabitable. Not like ours which was covered in oceans, and fresh water. Our land had huge sprawling cities, but also the greenest parts ever seen. Forests as far as the eye could see, even within the cities you could find green. We truly live in a paradise.

After a long journey we had finally arrived to find that the planet, this new one that we had been observing was indeed dead. It had died long before we arrived. The scorched land, the leveled cities, the abandoned areas that had once been residential areas, it all told a tale of distress, a tale of anger, and pain. It told a tale or disaster and tragedy. This planet died a slow painful death as did her inhabitants. But they brought it upon themselves. As far as we could tell her inhabitants had been lost, they killed each other through warfare.

"How tragic," I uttered, nearly a whisper while looking across the ruined wasteland of slag and debris. I couldn't help but think that they were probably beautiful creatures at one point in their existence. "Look at this." I pointed to the screen I had in front of me. "Look at this art, it was so beautiful. I don't think anything really survived sans a few primitive digital files stored away." I looked sorrowful at the fallout from such mindless destruction.

The xeno-biologist nodded, looking at her scanner output. "Yup it's a shame." She didn't seem as upset by the total destruction as myself. I guess I was probably being a little overly sensitive, but then again I'd like to think that emotions can be a good thing, especially when dealing with beings of lower intelligence. Sometimes they don't understand our intellect, and connecting emotionally is the only way to really communicate.

"Imagine. a species that evolves a trait to be so competitive that it kills itself, they develop such a strong hate and based on what? All I can seem to find is that they based their differences on some arbitrary lines, or the hue of the skin they were born with. It's truly astonishing that they would rather die, than admit they were all the same."

"Natural selection through competition is actually the fifth most common cause for intelligent life to evolve, we just don't think of it too often though, because those species usually die out before developing interstellar travel." She didn't even look up from her scanner "I don't know if you're aware of this, but at one point, our world was like that, brutal and uncivilized. We fought over everything these poor people probably did, and more. It was a lucky thing that we were able to reconcile our differences. As trivial as they seem to be now, in the moment, I understand, they were quite important."

"Mercy help us if one ever does make it to other stars. We'd be in no position to compete against that sort of race." I looked at her with a little fear and a little relief knowing she was right, any race that barbaric and violent would have killed themselves off long before ever reaching the capability of interstellar travel.

"Don't worry," She tried to reassure me. "The chances of that happening are practically zero."

"I know, I know." I paused and looked at her, she really was beautiful. One day I would make her my wife. One day when I had the courage. "Hey," She looked at me, "Thanks." She smiled and I felt like everything was ok.

"You're welcome, now lets get to this mission." I nodded in agreement and went back to my work. I shuddered upon doing research into their technology.

"These guys made it pretty close," I told her, "They had made it off their planet, they made it to the next planet from their sun. I believe it was named ares." I chucked a bit, and she looked at me. "Oh it's just that ares was the name of one of their deities. He was, and this is fairly ironic, the god of war." This made her let out a little chuckle. These people worshiped a god of war. There really was no hope for them.

We landed, the other ships in our fleet landed and we began scouring the planet for any materials that could be salvaged. And any life forms that could possibly be saved.

We found some a few unique creatures that were subdued and placed on ships. Our research was long and tiring, but we were finding that this planet had plenty of resources. We would have to send our massive mining and hauling ships here to retrieve the materials.

We had no idea that our worst nightmare would soon come true. It would seem that we were wrong about the life on this planet. We were wrong about them all killing themselves off. Deep beneath the cracked and charred ruins of the planet a certain system began responding to the presence of life on the surface above. One light clicked on, and then another. Thousands upon thousands of lights turned on, glowing warmly in the surrounding darkness. And above each one, a message appears:

Advanced military cryogenic resuscitation chamber: Activating

It took maybe a matter of six hours from when the first chamber began running for them all to be fully functional, and another six for those beings to have us completely surrounded. They carried very primitive weaponry, but we only had what was believed to be needed for animals without the ability of higher level thinking. They wiped out half of the total crew immediately. These monsters slaughtered my friends, and with no provocation, they were met with no resistance and still viciously murdered them.

The rest of us. We were taken as slaves, forced to take apart and rebuild our ships, forced to give them plans to build our ships. We were forced to teach them how to build, work on, and pilot these ships. We did what they asked in return for one ship and the ability to return to our world. we should have known they were lying, we should have known that they would never let us leave. We've been here for many, many years. We watched as they perfected using our technology. We watched as they weaponized it.

We realize now and perhaps always knew, but were too selfish and scared for our own safety to accept it, but we have doomed ourselves. And our species, they would take over our paradise. After decades of imprisonment they finally let us leave in one ship as they promised this was not an act of kindness. How blind could we be, they let us leave, and we led them straight to our home world. all we could do is cry out in pain as we watched them destroy every living person. They took their nuclear technology and infused it with our own advanced computers, and guidance.

Once they wiped out our people they used our technology. They used our antimatter, something that we never dreamed of weaponizing and they created warheads, the likes of which we had never encountered. Once they had completely perverted all of our peaceful technology they fully inhabited our planet calling the rest of their filthy kind to join the ones already here. Then they set their sites for a neighboring star. We had no chance to warn the planets that they were coming.

We cannot be forgiven for what we have unleashed on our home planet, on our solar system. We cannot be forgiven for the destruction they will unleash upon the galaxy. If you believe in a god... I suggest you begin praying.

-CHINADOLL84-

This was a blog that had seemed to appear out of nowhere in the late oh fives, it had a couple thousand followers, but nothing too big. It would have been another piece of work that had faded into obscurity, if not for the subject matter, as it was fairly short, the narrative it tells is terrifying, I could not imagine someone going through this. The blog user-name was; Chinadoll84.

11/10/2005

Hello, good morning and welcome to my blog. Please allow me to introduce myself and really explain what this whole thing is going to be about. My name is China, I'm 21 and I have a daughter, who's name is Chloe. The reason that I've created this blog is so I can get my story out there, I think something is going on with my daughter and I want to document it. She just turned five years old yesterday and that's when the most recent event happened. This one I managed to witness with my own eyes, but let me back up a little and give you the full back story on Chloe.

None of the other parents in my area will allow their children around her. And to be honest I don't blame them. They tell me it's not her, it's just the situation. Well the situation is that whenever she is alone with another child, that child ends up being hurt, sometimes no so bad, occasionally it was pretty severe. But it always seemed to be an accident. She was just bad luck. Something deep down told me it was more than that, screamed that Chloe was to blame. She's my daughter though, how can I suspect my five year old baby girl of any wrong doing? How could I suspect her of hurting other children.

So the play-dates got fewer and farther between, day-cares wouldn't take her, I had to find a private babysitter. But I did all that graciously, I loved my daughter. Now I should get back to the incident yesterday. It was at her birthday party, I managed to get the parents to allow their kids to come over, I guess the parents figured if there's a large group nothing could really happen. Well when it was time for cake we called them in. Most of the kids were already inside before I could finish my sentence.

I began cutting the cake when I noticed Chloe was missing, I walked to the back door to look for her. I found her. It was just her and the neighbor boy, outside, she was on the little slide she had and she called him to come up. I thought that was so sweet she wanted to slide down with him. What I saw then, turned my blood cold. When the boy got to the top of the slide, before he could sit, she jerked around and pushed his little feet out from under him. He lunged forward, smacking his face on the slide then falling backwards onto the ground.

I rushed out there to help the boy and Chloe was visibly surprised, she looked at me as if silently admitting what she just did. I rushed the boy into the house and called an ambulance, he broke his little nose when he hit the slide. The ambulance took the boy away and the party pretty much broke up, just leaving her and i. We sat in silence for a good long while, I had no idea what to say, I know what I saw. She purposely injured that other child. She called him up with malicious intent. My sweet little girl. This couldn't be true. After several minutes, I managed to eek out one word. "Why?"

She just stared at me in silence, a sinister little smile crept across her face but she said nothing. It became tense, and uncomfortable, I couldn't look at her any more. I got up and walked away to gather my thoughts.

11/25/2005

Welcome back to the blog, it's been about two weeks, I haven't posted because nothing noteworthy happened, that is until yesterday. It was thanksgiving. The family had gotten together we were reminiscing and just having a good time, the kids were playing, I was keeping a close eye on Chloe, as I always do when there are other children around us. She played like a normal child. Everything was going off without a hitch, and I began to feel like maybe I was just a little crazy, maybe it was all in my head. I allowed myself to relax and enjoy the get together. The smell of the turkey wafted from the kitchen, throughout the house. It smelled heavenly.

When the time came we all sat down for dinner hungry and mouth watering I wanted to dig in so bad. But grandma would be furious if we ate without saying grace, so we all joined hands and waited for her to start. She began to say grace and we all bowed our heads. When that was finished we began eating. My brother joey was, for lack of a better term, a glutton and he was raising his children the same way. The lord know diabetes will probably take that whole family. I bring this up because his thirteen year old boy was inhaling his food, I couldn't tell if he was chewing or not. On a particularly large bite, he started choking. His dad jumped into action and dislodged the food item with great profession, I assume this isn't the first time he's had to. None of this really seems worth telling you but believe me it is. When my nephew began to turn blue, before his father got to him. I glanced around the table to see if anyone could do something and I caught a glimpse of Chloe, my daughter, she was staring right at him, she looked as if she could hardly contain her laughter.

12/27/2005

Two days after Christmas, she was excited and happy to open her presents. Slowly as the morning progressed though, her demeanor changed. She started becoming a bit uninterested then almost annoyed. I guessed that I didn't get her what she wanted, but I got her a lot of nice stuff. It was more than I had ever gotten growing up. The next morning when I woke up, and went to wake her up, I stepped into her room, immediately fire shot up through my leg and I hit the ground, hard. I had stepped on something jagged and sharp. I cursed as I slowly made my way back to my feet and turned the light on. Every single item that she had gotten for Christmas was broken and thrown on the floor, pieces with sharp edges left just inside the doorway. I always walk through the house barefoot in the mornings. And I wake her up without the light so she can gently wake up... did she do this on purpose to hurt me? I asked her why she broke her toys and why they were on the floor. She flashed me her most innocent smile. "I don't know mommy, I don't remember doing it." I knew she was lying.

1/31/2006

Hello and welcome back to my Blog. After the last incident I have become kind of scared of my daughter. I don't know why she wanted to hurt me, or wants to hurt me. I haven't really left the house, other than for work. I watch her play, I watch her eat, I'm always just watching her. Nothing happens, she seems to be an average little girl. Once again I began to think that maybe it is in my head. I feel a little silly for being scared of her. I'm sorry for that. This will probably be my last blog post.

3/4/2006

It's become escalated, she wanted to watch something violent on television, and I of course told her no. she pleaded and threw a little fit. In response to her fit, I scooped her off the floor, I was going to let her get her anger out in her bedroom and she could come back out when she had calmed down. Half way down the hall she sunk her teeth into my arm. She bit down as hard as her little jaws would allow. I dropped her in the hall way and through her tears she smirked at me. I had to disinfect and bandage my arm as she broke the skin pretty severely. She picked herself off of the floor and started walking towards her room, she stopped at a picture of her and I on the wall, climbed on the little stand to grab it, and launched it at the opposing wall shattering it. She then calmly went into her room and shut the door. This was just a few hours ago.

I'm so scared, I really don't know what to do with her, I cant call the cops, what would I tell them? I cant exactly fight back, she's only five. So to any of my readers out there, what would you do? I need advice! I'm at a loss, and if things get worse I have no idea what will happen

6/5/2009

I know it's been years since my last blog post, I'm sorry, my life has fallen apart and become a living hell. A couple days after the last incident I posted, she broke my nose. She wanted me to buy her something and I refused so she slammed her head into my face. I was bleeding and in tears, it hurt so bad, and she was laughing hysterically. Her true side came out. I took her to a mental institution for children but they released her, she was a very good actress. She went through all of their tests, brilliantly, every question answered just like a typical five year old. It was that night that I had woken up. Something startled me and disturbed my sleep. I opened my eyes and there she was sitting Indian style on the foot of my bed, looking at me, almost as if contemplating. In her lap was a large butcher knife. "I'm trying to decide if I need you" the words came out very matter of factly, without emotion. "I guess you're useful, so, I can keep you around, try not to outlive that usefulness though *mom.*" She got up and hopped off the bed, she started to walk away then stopped looked at me as if still trying to contemplate whether I should live, then finished walking out.

I became so distraught I was let go from my job, my life fell to pieces. My friends stopped calling, they stopped showing up to check on me. They stopped trying to contact me. I drove the rest of my family away from me. I've managed to alienate them all. If anyone found out how Chloe treats me, I don't want the getting hurt trying to step in.

It's gotten so bad, that I became a prisoner in my own home. She's gotten much older, much more sadistic and brutal. She's stronger than I am, she's demanding, and she hit's me. She's cut me, it's become like a fucked up abusive relationship. The worst thing of all of this though, it's that she's become much more self reliant. The less she needs me the more scared for my life I become. She's begun looking at me like an old dog that needs to be put down. I don't know how long I'm going to survive. I need to fight back.

6/7/2009

Tonight is the night. When she's sleeping I'm going to try to do something, maybe escape, maybe kill her. Hell I don't know, but something has to be done! She's going to kill me if I don't do something, and she's going to kill me soon. She... she came home today, covered in blood, I don't know if she's torturing animals or humans, I cant be sure. But I know I'm not long for this world if I stay here! I will update you all when I can. Please pray for me.

This is where this story ultimately ends. This was the last post ever posted on that blog, there was never any word about what happened, if China made it out of the house or not. The blog was taken down in twenty-fifteen, and there has been no further word about China, or Chloe.

-I DIDN'T KILL HER-

Today-

I am in a police interrogation room. I've been talking to officers and detectives. They sent in a shrink at one point. They are asking me all these questions and I'm being as helpful as I can given the situation. I don't know what else to do at this point. I'm sitting across from a grizzled detective. He keeps looking at some file that's in his hand, and then back at me. I'm not sure how any of this works. Is he waiting for me to talk, or is he trying to figure out what to say? I broke the tense silence. "I did not kill my daughter, I just didn't. I don't know how to make you guys understand that! I loved my daughter Miranda She was my world. I don't know where she got that bottle." I was distressed on the verge of weeping. "I get that I these times, in these tragedies you have to look at the closest people to the victim. I get that." I paused in an effort to contain myself. "But that's what this was, a tragedy. I should have seen it coming, given everything else that has happened in her young life, but I just wasn't a strong enough father for her." The detective shifted his position but remained silent. The look in his eyes changed, at first I felt like he was a pit-bull ready to chew into me, but now he had eyes of a puppy. Looking at me with sorrow and empathy. "I wasn't strong enough of a father." I repeated before breaking down and weeping. "I wasn't there for her, I didn't see the signs, and she took her life." I was outright bawling at this point "can-can we be done here? Can I go? I have things that I need to take care of." He nodded

"I truly am sorry for your loss Mr. Biggs, I have a

daughter myself, and I could not imagine being in your situation." He gave me a friendly handshake and a sympathetic look. "If there is anything that I can do for you, please don't hesitate to call." I took the business car he had extended to me, thanked him and headed for the door.

Yesterday-

Today is the day that all my work over the last year pays off. The culmination of everything that's been building since that day. One year ago, my wife was killed. She was always insisting on going out, she loved partying and having a good time. She was such an amazing woman and wanted to experience everything that life had to offer. I loved her for that. On one Saturday evening she begged me to go to this fancy new dance club that recently opened. But I was exhausted, I had worked a sixty hour week, and just wanted to have a beer and relax. She understood and asked if I minded if she went. I didn't, a little peace and quiet is what I needed. So she went dancing and I settled in with a six pack and some television.

I was two beers down and about forty five minutes in when Miranda came in the house, it was eleven so I didn't really pay too much attention. She started rooting around in the kitchen where her cell rang, I winced a little, I knew exactly what was coming.

"Hellooooo guuuuurl!" It started from there the conversation got louder and louder. I turned up the TV a few times, but it didn't seem to help. She never really thought about others. I got off the couch and strolled towards the kitchen, stopping in the doorway. I stood there, and waited for her to notice me, this seemed futile, she was in her own little world. I cleared my throat loudly, loud enough to get her attention over her conversation in her phone. She spun quickly startled because he didn't notice me until then.

"It is eleven, I had a hard week paying for that damn phone, would you mind keeping it down a little." I asked. It was a question but it was directed in the same manner as a demand.

"Oh I'm so sorry daddy, of course." She was chipper about it. As I turned toward the living room I heard her telling the person on the other end that I said she was too loud and she would just text them. Thank god, she was going to keep it down.

I went back to my television, and polished off the other four. I looked at the clock and it was midnight so I went to bed. The next morning, that was the morning that I had began to put this plan together. I woke up to my phone shattering the serenity of my bedroom. It was jarring and pulled me right out of my sleep. I scrambled for my phone, and hit the button. "Mr Biggs?" The voice called through my phone "I'm sorry, I'm looking for a Mr Biggs."

"This is Mr Biggs." I was hesitant to give any information, but a name couldn't hurt.

"Mr Biggs, it's regarding your wife. Can you get to the hospital?" My mind immediately began racing, I barely heard what the man was saying. I was already on my way to the hospital. I got to the emergency room and told them who I was looking for. I was informed that she was in operation. I waited for her. I paced the room, I started praying to god, I made a few phone calls. I felt so helpless. I got information about what had happened. It was a shooting, some guy just showed up at the club, when the man tried to get in the bouncer stopped him, that's when he pulled the weapon and began firing. My wife was one of the people who got hit by a bullet. the man got into a gunfight with police, and the coward decided to just shoot himself instead of letting the cops apprehend him. After a couple of hours later a doctor appeared in the door way and called my name. I met him at the door and he talked to me. He explained that the bullet had done too much damage on the way in, and was lodged in a place that it could not be removed. She died on the operating table. I was distraught and broken. I didn't know how I'd be able to pick up the pieces and move on. I didn't know if I could.

When I got home, Miranda was waiting there, she had\ gotten the news about her mother and she looked at me for strength. She was looking at me for answers, and support. "what are we going to do daddy?" She asked through tears. "what am I going to do, why did this happen?" I couldn't believe how selfish she was I had lost my wife, the reason that I wake up everyday!

"I don't know god dammit! I don't know what you're going to do." I snapped at her. And she began to wail. Every day it got worse. She got worse. She became more and more bratty, more and more annoying, always talking back to me. She became more and more needy. She became reliant on me for everything. She quit her job, she stopped going out with her friends. She was always at the house. she was always needing something from me, she always needed a piece of me. Well what about my needs? What about what I need? I had gotten fed up with her, I started staying out of the house more. I snapped at her when she tried to talk to me. I was short and yelled often. She said it was hell trying to live with me. Someone should have told her what it's like to live with little miss god damned princess, it wasn't exactly a walk in the park.

Truth be told, I never even wanted kids. I was happy

without any of them. It was my wife who wanted to get pregnant and have a kid, and god, I couldn't tell that woman no. I went along, I had a baby with her, for her, I did my best to love the child. But it was because of her. Then she left me. This whole thing was just dumped in my lap, I didn't know how to raise teenager. And for the rest of her life, I was going to be expected to take care of her. I couldn't do it. I didn't ask for any of this. I never wanted any of this. It just wasn't fair.

Well over this last year I've managed to wear her down, I've done my best to slowly whittle away at her self esteem. I gradually broke her little spirit. She was soft, and weak. It really didn't take that much to make her fall apart. It was pathetic, she was pathetic. I didn't even have to come outright and be blunt. All I had to do was make subtle comments, ignore her when she needed support, or casually blame her when something went bad in her life. The real piece de resistance was cutting off the wi-fi when she really seemed to need it, I cut that little bitch off from the thing she seemed to love the most. I cut her off from the people and support that she found online. As she drifted away from her friends I slowly convinced her that they don't like her. She spiraled into depression pretty quick, and I did my best to keep her there.

So now here I stand, a fresh bottle of whiskey just sitting on the counter, beckoning to be drank, along with an unmarked bottle of very strong narcotic painkillers. I know that she's at the breaking point, so with opportunity I'm sure that selfish little brat will finally end it. Just to be sure though, gave her one more little push. A note with the items I left for her, one I'd have to grab before dialing the police tonight;

"Why don't you do the world a favor and join your mother."

-Love Daddy

-ANGELS AND DEMONS-

I fear life. I fear life so much that I often think about killing myself. Now before you dismiss me as overly emotional, I don't mean that in a depression sort of way. What I mean is that there are things in this life, things that most people cant see. I don't know what exactly you would call them. But I guess the closest thing I could say would be spirit's... no, angels. Angels, and demons would be the best way to describe them.

I see them constantly, they are always following people. They're always talking to the people they're always following, always talking. It's almost as if I'm in a weird show where the angel and devil pop up onto people's shoulders, but this is much more sinister. The angels and demons didn't seem to be as light hearted as they did in movies, they way they looked at each other. The hatred in their exchanging stares. The anger was so tense you could feel it. It was terrifying. But my situation it wasn't always like this though. I used to be a normal girl, I even used to be happy.

The start of all this, it was so subtle at first, a quick spot in the corner of my eye, a person casting two shadows. Almost as if there were two light sources, even though there was only one. But then when I would make a double take, they were gone. This strange phenomenon slowly increased, and yet they (that is the angels and demons) never seemed to notice me. I really wasn't sure what to make of these entities. They didn't take notice of me, so I wasn't sure if they were even real, or just a figment of my imagination. I contemplated going to see someone about it. I thought about going to see a doctor, or a psychiatrist. Slowly as they became more visible, I began seeing them standing by people, I began to see them whispering. But still, they didn't seem to notice me, and the people they whisper to, don't seem to notice them either.

One day something changed though, something turned very, very wrong. One day I was sitting with my little brother in the living room. He was watching something on TV I wasn't paying much attention. I let out a small gasp when I seen one of the spirit's, a bad one, a demon. It was talking to him, to my little brother. I couldn't hear what he was saying but I could see the evil in it's eyes. I looked around and saw no good spirit, no angel. I didn't know what that meant, I didn't have long to contemplate it though. All of the sudden my little brother just stood up and pushed the TV over. The screen cracked, the whole thing made a weird noise and then it just cut out.

I was in a stunned silence. I just sat there frozen. couldn't believe what he'd just done he's always been such a great kid. This was so out of character for him. He looked up at me with wide eyes, he seemed almost as shocked as I was at what he just did. The 'demon' gave a small twisted smile. The smallest noise, a tiny eep escaped my throat when I realized the implications of what just happened. That's when the bad one looked over towards me, through me, into me. He stared intensely the smile still on his face. I was terrified. He seemed to revel in that. He was the first one to notice me. but not the last.

That was quite a while ago, and I've grown used to them looking at me, the good ones the bad ones, they never do anything. They never talk to me, they never make any moves towards me. They just watch as I pass by. They know I see them, I don't think they really know what to make of my gift, to tell the truth I really haven't figured it out yet. I just try to live my life the best I can, I avoid the people that don't have any of the angels with them. The most curious thing is though, that I've never had any of them talk to me, none of them whisper to me. I supposed it's because I can see them, and they know that they cant influence me the way that they do to the others, that's my best guess. But still I have to wonder why. I wonder why often. Why they don't talk to me, why they're so fascinated by me, why I was given this gift.

As I said in the beginning, I've become terrified of life, and the thing that's got me terrified to be alive any more, is that I think they're planning something... something big. The bad ones, I mean, the demons. I've watched as the good ones slowly die out. I don't know what's happening to them. All I really know is that everyday when I wake up, and pull myself out of bed, I see more and more bad ones, and less good ones. I feel so scared, I'm afraid of what they're planning. It's gotten to the point where I'm seeing demons that are not even with people they just wait for me. they are constantly watching me. they're not watching with the same expression as they used to either. It's not pleasure, or curiosity. They look at me the way they and the angels would look at each other. I'm so terrified of what they might do to me that I've been contemplating taking my own life. I've tied at least a hundred nooses, I could do it in my sleep. I could do it behind my back, I could probably do it with my feet. I've thought of every possible way to end it. Pills, alcohol, driving into a tree, cutting my wrists.

As I stare down at the gun in my hand, my mind races, what could they want? Why are the good ones dying off like that, and where are they going? Who's going to protect humanity from the bad ones? Who's going to persuade people into doing good? How, and why, are things becoming so out of balance. I look up and there are four of them standing in the room I'm in waiting watching, sick and twisted smiles on their faces, the burning hatred in their eyes. They've never been in my room before, the shock nearly sent me tumbling out the back of the chair I was sitting on.

One of them takes his first step towards me. I will not let them get their hands on me, I will not let them use me, if I'm going to die, I'm going to die on my own terms. I placed the barrel in my mouth I taste the metal, look up and whisper "I'm coming home." And squeezed the trigger.

"She's been on the machine for far too long." The doctor stared at the young girls parents, sympathy and kindness in his eyes sadness and regret in his voice. "We need to take her off the life support, that's the only shot she has for waking up, the risk is high if she doesn't wake up… she'll die." He paused and looked at the couple standing before him, "If we don't take her off," he continued. "Then she will be on the machine forever. By shutting down the machine, it could shock her body into working on it's own, and the mind should be able to follow suit."

Her parents sat with the child for what seemed like ages, talking and praying. The decision was hard, how can parents be asked to make such a final decision? How can they be expected to take that risk. After days of constant discussion and crying they finally had managed to come to a heart breaking decision. The decision to pull the plug. The doctor prepared the girl, and slowly began shutting down the life support. When done her body jerked, a deep breath escaped her lips, and she fell limp. The girl's mother distraught with guilt and a terrible pain broke down and wept, her father had to remain strong. But he was closer to the girl and what he heard when she exhaled… it stayed with him for many years after her passing.

He could swear her final words were;

"I'm coming home."

-THE PHOTOGRAPH-

There is a particular picture floating around the internet. This picture shows a middle aged woman, mid to late thirties, she is standing with a young child, about ten. She's wearing a old fashioned black dress, the child is a fairly typical young boy. You could almost imagine him fidgeting right before the camera snapped. The photo is in black and white, although it's more of a sepia due to aging before it was transferred into the digital realm. It's a very old picture and if the original hasn't deteriorated completely, than it would be one of few of that particular line that is left in tact. When gazing at this particular picture most people feel unease, anxiety, or even outright fear, or sadness. They cant really pinpoint why, and the most common reasoning given is; "There's something wrong with the child," and other statements along that line this is more accurate than they know.

You see, the woman in this picture. is not the child's mother, or aunt, or related to the kid at all. This pic is the last picture of that child. Alive anyways. This woman was sweet and kind. She was always there with a kind word, a hug and emotional support. She would move into town and instantly become friends with, well everyone. Oh how charming she was, and when she got dressed and made up, she was beautiful. She'd have many suitors, but never married or even had a date, she was a devout christian and was waiting for god to tell her when the right man has come. While she was lonely, she was convinced that god had a plan for her, and she trusted him.

She was an experienced nanny, and had done a little bit

of nursing. so she had the skills to quickly get hired to take care of children from one of the befriended families. Being the kind hearted woman she was, she was easily trusted. She was a great house keeper and the house always smelled of cookies, cakes, pies, and other such delicious treats. The woman seemed to be perfect. And the children adored her and she would be considered a part of the family. No-one ever notices anything is off. At first.

After about a month goes by of her being a nanny to the children the little ones start to become distant they almost seem like they didn't want to be alone with her anymore, they begin to act almost as if they were scared. They didn't know why they felt this anxiety (or they did and lied about it.) It turns out what was happening is every night is that she would come over to the families house, and back then doors were never locked. She'd come in real quiet and watch the children sleep sometimes for hours, she adored the children, she loved them oh how she loved the children! Sometimes they would stir and occasionally wake up, she would convince them to sleep again.

As I said she loved the children but it was more than normal, she didn't just love the children she became obsessed with them, but it was this love I believe that caused what would happen next.

As the children grew distant she wanted them to love\ her even more, she craved it. This woman would pick her favorite child if the family had multiple, and would watch that particular child every night for about a week maybe more. She would slip into the house, and stand near the bed. Occasionally stroking their hair, adjusting their blanket, or some other way of making minor contact.

Then when she saw that the time was right and she

was ready she would gently lift the child out of bed, whispering and gently singing so as too lull the child back into slumber as she carried him away. She would take the child down the road to her car and drive out of town to a motel. This is where she would keep the child tied up. She would leave the child here so she could then show up for work the next day and be just as confused, shocked, and panicked, as anyone that the child's gone missing. This is the last time anyone would see her. The woman would leave her employer's home that day and after this she would have a picture taken of her with the child.

After the picture was taken, this is when it gets, it gets hard to talk about. I'm not sure what exactly brought about her madness but, I'd like to think that whatever it was must have been immensely painful and traumatizing. I don't want to think that someone could be this evil and heartless for no reason. I don't want to believe that humanity could hold this much evil in their heart.

After her picture, she would take the child away from the town, driving for days on end to find what she needed. She was looking for empty or abandoned buildings such as a decrepit barn, or something of that sort. In the case of this photograph, she came across an old shack in the middle of nowhere. This would be perfect. There were miles of empty fields where she could do what she needed to do.

She would chain the child up and hoist him up side down by his ankles. He would then put a small puncture in a child's jugular forcing them to slowly bleed out into a bathtub, bucket, or any other suitable container for the blood. As the child bled she then slice the palm of her hand open. When enough of her own blood had oozed out, she would begin to smear it on the child saying, "we are now one. You are blood of my blood and I am blood of your blood." Once the body was drained she would take a very sharp knife slice from the bottom of the stomach all the way to the neck with the precision of a surgeon the internal organs of the body would spill into the container. Now drained of blood corpse wide open, she would snap another photo.

The photo of her and the child along with the photo of the corpse would be sent to the parents of the child enclosed in the envelope would also be a letter. While I don't know every detail of the letter, I can tell you that in certain parts she would write how she loved the child. She would confess that that's all she wanted was the child's heart in any other context that would be very loving she was also enclose the directions to the place where she had committed the atrocities. When the police search, they would find the child's body but in no case did they ever find the child's heart.

-NEVER HAVE I EVER-

I was hanging out with some old friends that I haven't seen since high school. Back then we were the best of friends. We did just about everything together, and we were inseparable. We all thought that we were gonna be best friends for the rest of our lives. So many big plans made for college, we'd get into the same frat, party every night! God we were stupid kids, but it was fun to dream. Well it's been about eight years since the group disbanded as most of us went to college. Problem was, that we got accepted into different colleges. Staying in touch was harder that first thought. Between studying, working, and the occasional party, there really wasn't too much time to get a hold of old friends. And definitely no time to road trip to go see them.

Everything seemed to turn out ok for each of us though. We all seemed to be doing rather well. Everyone was fairly successful in their own definition. Me personally, I had a good job, it paid well, and I didn't hate the work. I had a gorgeous wife. A nice house and a fast car. A couple of the guys were single a couple had wives, one guy had a whole family. In all, even though we lost touch, and that sucked, we were all pretty happy.

Well putting it all together took a few months of planning and face-booking, schedule rearranging and group conversations. But we somehow managed to get all six of us back together! We would only be able to come together for a three day weekend, so it was decided we would go to Vegas. I booked a rather large suite in one of the fancier casino hotels, and booked my flight. This was going to be perfect!

The day had finally arrived, I was extremely happy, albeit a little nervous, I hadn't seen these guys in years, what if they changed, and I didn't know them any more? What if they haven't changed and they're still as immature as we all were when we were younger? Which would be worse? I couldn't decide. When I met up with them in the lobby of the hotel, immediately we were back in high school. Not in the sense that we were immature brats like I feared, but in the fact that our friendship was as strong as ever. I had my group back together and we just picked right up where we had left off. Sure we were teasing one another, and poking fun but that's something we'll probably never grow out of. We were laughing talking and swapping stories. Getting into proverbial pissing contests as men often do. And then reminiscing about the old days. We talked about college, told each other of our 'sexual conquests' I'm sure about seventy five percent of the sex talk was bullshit, but that's what you get when you put six male egos in a room together. The weekend flew by way too quickly, but it was a ton of\ fun. We gambled, we drank, we acted like men. Which when being married can sometimes be more difficult. On that last night we were all just winding down with a few beers and catching up on all the things we've done since high school. College was pretty wild, although not all of us went, so our experiences were fairly differed. It was interesting to hear what everyone was up to, and what kind of trouble they managed to get their selves into without the group. Our swapping of war stories soon turned into a game of 'never have I ever.'

If you've never heard of this game, please allow me to explain. Someone says something they've never done. Example; I've never put ketchup on scrambled eggs. At this point anyone who has done it takes a drink. It's a fairly simple game, and the more adventurous one is, the more they wind up drinking.

Well it was all typical guy stuff at first never have I ever had a threesome, never have I ever gone skydiving, never have I ever hired a prostitute, et cetera. As time went on, and we got more and more drinks in us, the lips got looser and our little game, it started to get a little darker. "Never have I ever been in a real fist fight." most of us took a sip. "Never have I ever hit a car and took off," a couple sips. "Never have I ever hit a woman." A few more sips, silence and judgment filled the room, as the six of us exchanged uneasy glances. I'm not sure if any of us really knew where to go from here. I'm not sure if some of these friendships would be able to be saved after this game was over. I tried to break the tension a little bit with a joke topic. "Well I've never killed anyone at least." All eyes fell on me, as the five men before me raised their bottles to their lips and began to drink.

My eyes shot open, confused, shaking and drenched in a cold sweat I struggle to gain my bearings. I shake out the fog, and try to figure out where I'm at. All at once it hit's me, I must have been having a terrible dream. I cant remember what exactly I dreamt about, but now I'm lying in my comfy bed, next to my sleeping wife. I struggle to remember what the dream was, but the longer that I'm in this world, the harder it becomes to reach back into that one. I shrug it off, and decide it's just better to get ready for my job. Stumbling out of my bedroom I try to make my way into the bathroom, feeling weak and shaky as if my body did not get the message that it's awake now. I manage to shut the door behind me, and feel around to find and eventually flip on the light switch.

I seem to be having trouble remembering the layout of

my own place this morning. It's miracle I didn't wake my wife up, all the noise I was making. As I undress for a shower I catch a glimpse of red on my shirt, 'ketchup' the word shoots into my head, but I don't remember having anything with ketchup last night, as a matter of fact, I don't remember anything that happened last night. I examine my shirt to find that the front of it has been painted red with blood, a quick look, reveals no cuts, scrapes, or wounds on my person that would cause such a stain. Shaking once again I call out with a weak voice to my wife. No answer.

Stepping out I flip a switch by the door, light floods the room, and immediately I see, I'm not in my house. I wasn't in my bed, and that was not my wife lying next to me. From the way she's dressed, my best guess is that she's probably an escort she was gorgeous. Pouty lips, decent perky breasts, long legs...I Knew I must have been with her last night, but cheating on my wife was the least of my problems though.

The woman's body was beaten, badly. She had bruises and contusions on her face, arms and torso. Her arms and legs were tied, the ropes left severe rope burns from her struggling, and she had a scarf jammed in her mouth. She was dead. Her body had been sliced open from the top to the bottom of her torso. Accompanied by several stab wounds. a knife lay by her head on the pillow, covered in blood. Everything was covered in blood. The sheets, the bed. So many thoughts began running through my brain. What am I going to do? Do I call the police? This is probably my fault, I'd spend the rest of my life in jail. Do I run? Do I hide the body? My evidence is all over the room, I'll never manage to get away with this. Standing here looking at the dead girl lying in this motel room, I can see my entire life crumbling before my eyes. As I begin to lose my shit, on the edge of breaking down and weeping. Mourning the loss of everything I held dear. I notice a shot glass full of what I assume is whiskey with a note it read; "Never have I ever ... take your drink sir."

What have I done?

-BEAUTIFUL-

I stood there, waiting, in the middle of a small street, with fields on both sides of me, containing gorgeous flowers, I couldn't help but to wonder what they were, as I was not familiar with the types. They were such nice deep shades of blues, reds, purples, yellows, pinks and more. The road was an old dirt road, like from the time before they really had cars, it was quite nice it reminded me of the old times when the street belonged to everyone. The sun was shining down on us, the rays felt good on my face. There wasn't a cloud to be seen in the sky.

The line was, well it was much shorter than I could have ever expected. At the front of the line I saw there was a man in a suit, he sat behind a desk he was patiently checking everyone in. Yes there was a desk outside, but I'll get to that in a minute. It seemed as if it were a very formal ordeal, I couldn't believe it. I always expected... well I don't know, chaos, disorder, at least excitement, or anxiety, some kind of emotion. Everyone just stood in the line like waiting at the DMV.

It was all very ordinary, and I guess giving the fact that I was dead, makes that in itself extraordinary. The gates lie in front of me, wonderful magnificent gates, made of gold, and platinum. They were decorated with precious gems such as diamonds, rubies, and other metals and jewels I had never seen before. When it was my turn, I finally got to the front of the line, the suited man looked me up and down as if sizing me up. He had a blank expression, so I couldn't help but wonder if he was impressed or disappointed in the man who stood before him now. I said nothing. Soon he started typing away on his computer, when he shifted in his chair I saw a single silvery feather fall from somewhere underneath his black suit and flutter to the ground. it was so elegant and wonderful. He was focused on his computer, only glancing at me occasionally, I don't think he much cared for me at all, but I still said nothing. My mind wandered, I wanted to know what was on that laptop he was typing on, I was curious to know what he thought of me. I had many questions about this place, and about where I was going. I didn't believe him to be in a talkative mood though, so I stood quietly and patiently

Looking behind me, I see the line has grown a bit longer than when I first arrived, I was still in disbelief, I really thought the line would have been longer. The tension I felt between the man in the suit and myself was broken by him, when he finally stood up and reaches out offering his hand to me. I reached forward leaning in just a hair and grabbed his. his grip was firm, I matched it, and we shook. He pointed me towards the gates, and they opened just a little bit, just enough for a single person to walk through. I took a few steps towards them, before turning to the man. I thanked him for his kind service, and patience with me. He nodded and gestured for me to move on. I think whatever he found on his laptop did indeed impress him, and earned his respect.

Once I stepped inside those gates, I was greeted with sights more wondrous and amazing than I could imagine. Beautiful curtains made from the finest silk, with gold woven throughout, hung on the walls. Chandeliers that were cut from the most radiant crystals, shone the most glorious light down. The floors were tiled white with ivory, spiral staircases only dreamed of, lined with ebony, the contrast was breath taking! Walking through, I couldn't help but admire the paintings, these were finer than anything ever dreamt of on earth, as my eyes were pulled from piece to masterful peace, I could not contain myself and broke into tears. I wept as I stood in the presence of artwork that would make a Van Gogh look like a child's macaroni art. A Rembrandt would be nothing more than a spilled tube of paint in comparison.

I composed myself and continued my journey onward, in my path was a most vibrant floor rug, with reds, purples, blues, greens, pinks, and colors, colors that did not exist in the physical universe. I did not want to walk over it. Each step I took was more alluring than the last. As I stood at the edge of the rug, about to walk around it, a man came down, gently floating on silver wings, another, and another came down, the wings shimmering, so lovely. The light from the crystals above our heads, gently dancing off each and every feather.

I caught the eyes of one of these men, and he flashed me a warm smile, and held out his hand. He must have read my apprehension to walk on the rug, all over my face. I took it, and he led me through, to a solid oak door. Needless to say the carving on the door was more elegant than I can find words to describe. The door slowly opened and he led me through, it shut behind us.

The hallway that we stepped into was just as exquisite as the room before it. The difference is where as the last room smelt of jasmine, and honey, this hall smelled of iron. A short walk in, and the man, the angel that I was following, lifted himself off the ground. I continued on the floor wondering what he had done to be here. His wings so beautiful, he himself so amazing. I walked through blood just a small amount beginning to accumulate at first, but it got deeper as I walked. Suddenly the screams filled my ears, and I was all to quickly reminded of where I was. Even over the screaming, the torturing and pain that I could hear. Even over the smell of iron, the smell of blood... I never expected Hell to be this beautiful.

-THE WAKE-

If you're traveling through the Midwest, around autumn. If you happen to find yourself on some deserted almost abandoned back highway. If you happen across a particular but generally non nondescript park, right around midnight. I would caution you, to be careful but go ahead and pull in. The gate will most likely be closed and locked but you can park in front of it, and walk in. If you have with one with you, bring a set of black clothes and change in the change rooms. If you don't have them available it's not necessary but it couldn't hurt.

When you come out of the restroom, walk towards the middle of the park. Keep your eyes out and you will see that there will be an old man with olive colored skin and curly dark brown hair. He has an interesting looking mustache, but no beard. This man will be selling hot dogs in a cart. (now while it may strike you as odd being that it's so late, this man is harmless, I promise) go ahead and order a hot dog, this is important as you are on the cusp of another realm, think of this man as sort of a gate keeper. Once you order the dog, decorate it how you'd like and finish it. The man will thank you for your patronage.

He will then attempt to chat you up. He's a very interesting man and he has some excellent things to say and advice to give, so lend him an ear and a few moments of your time, you wont be disappointed. When he's finished, he will say something a little confusing to you at first. He will apologize for your loss saying, "I'm sure the wake will be nice." Don't question him, don't ask him what he means, simply thank him for his kindness and walk away.

As you begin to walk away you may notice the most peculiar thing. No matter what the weather was like when you arrived, even if it was bone dry and the sky was clear of any clouds. You'll find that a thick dense fog has managed to rolling, undetected. Looking around it will be hard to see anything, the fog is so thick you could cut it with a knife. Don't stop. Don't turn around. Keep walking forward. You have left your world, but have not quite reached your destination. This is an in between realm, and believe me you don't want to get lost here. If you look behind you you'll see nothing, even if you try to head back you'll find the hotdog vendor is gone, and the park seems to go on forever. Keep moving forward.

As you move, the fog will become lighter, and eventually you will be able to see the park again. That being said you may not recognize the place, as the place you just left. That's because it's not the same place, you will be standing in a graveyard at this point. You should see a funeral going on up ahead, walk quietly over to it.

As you approach try not to draw any attention to yourself. Silently slip into the crowd. Do not disturb any of the mourners, stand in the back, with your head lowered as if in prayer. You may or may not recognize those who stand in mourning. If you do say nothing, they do not recognize you.

At the end before lowering the deceased into the ground, they will open the casket one final time. Several of the people attending this funeral will go up to say a few final words to them, wait until they are done and walk up yourself and peer into the casket.

Now when you do look into the casket do not gasp, do not cry out, do not scream, do not make any kind of scene at all. When you look into the face of the dead you'll probably notice that the person in the casket looks like you, probably significantly older, maybe a parent or even a grandparent. But the resemblance to you in uncanny. In some cases you'll even notice that the person is roughly your age, and looks just like you. There's a reason for the similarity and I'm sure you have already guessed this but, this person is you. When everyone else has had a chance to go up, and has said their peace. Take your turn, walk up, bow your head as if praying and respectively leave. Again without drawing too much attention to yourself. Before walking away you do have to get permission to leave, for lack of a better term, the way you got permission to enter. This time you must talk to the priest performing the funeral, walk up to him, shake his hand tell him "Thank you father the service was lovely." He will accept your thanks, he may ask to pray for you. If he does ask, your going to want to let him. When he is finished he will tell you in a friendly manner that he doesn't want to see you again for a long time.

It is extremely important that, the whole time you're there, until you're in your car and pulling away from the park, that you be very non disruptive and respectful as not to draw any attention. You really don't want the forces that be to know you just attended your own funeral. The reward for doing this correctly is the knowledge of roughly your death date. You'll be able to gather from how old your corpse is, how old you'll be when you die. You can live life with no fear from here on out.

I believe that I should mention this, if they discover you while at your funeral, the consequences will be worse than death. One other warning, if when you look into the coffin. If the corpse is you, as in your age, and wearing the clothes you're currently wearing. It doesn't matter if you scream or make a scene.

They already know you're there.

-THE SHADOWS-

Have you ever glanced up from what you were doing or looked around real quick, and seen something out of the corner of your eye? Something off? Like a shadow, but when you look directly at it, it's gone? You probably just chock it up to a trick of the mind. For most people that's a good enough explanation, and it's best to just leave it alone. For others though, they get too curious for their own good. They look too deep into the abyss, and that is when things start to change for them. This story in particular is about a young woman by the name of Tiffany her story starts off as simple as any other, she was a typical sweet teenage girl. Just a few days removed from her fifteenth birthday.

Tiffany had always seen the shadows in the corner of her eyes, but like so many others, she ignored them. One day though she looked up real quick, and didn't see a shadow. It wasn't just a shadow at least, could have sworn that there was a person standing there at the edge of her vision. Just standing there, watching, waiting. It was gone in an instance as she turned to get a better look. Tiffany should have let it go, she should have let that be the end of it, but she didn't.

After that day she was hooked, she was constantly moving her eyes flicking them back and fort, in a psychotic attempt to possibly catch a glimpse of whatever it was she seen. Not being able to repeat the effect, she was becoming discouraged, and almost gave up. She lie sleeping one night when she heard someone call out to her, she shot up in bed, and for one split second she thought she saw something by her bed. She shot her eyes toward it, but as her vision swept across the room, the shadow stayed at the edge until ultimately it seemed to slip into her bedroom closet. She sprang out of bed and ran to the closet, but it was empty. She lied in bed the rest of the night, unable to sleep.

The following morning the first thing she did was hit the computer to do some research. She found all kinds of things out, but nothing of particular interest. She did not let that discourage her though, she kept looking, kept searching, and eventually she got good at catching them. It was always just a hint now and then, and always just a split second. Every time she caught one though, it always seemed surprised or angry to her. She kept looking.

Her life fell to pieces as she dug deeper and deeper into this. She went to antique book stores, contacted mediums, priests, and members of the church of Satan She was a young woman obsessed. Grades suffered, she alienated her family, began to argue with before ultimately ignoring her parents, she barely ate, or slept. Everyone she talked to gave her different answers about the shadow figures, this was frustrating but not enough to dissuade her. The glimpses she had were getting longer. She could get eyes on these figures for a full second at a time. They were human... humanoid.

She finally got an answer although she was not expecting it. While on the computer for the thirtieth hour straight, her phone rag, and she nearly fell out of her chair as the ring screamed through the silence. She answered it.

"Hello, we have never met, but I'm father Bauer The lord our god spoke with me, he told me to call you, and put a stop to what you're doing. There is another world, an alternate dimension if you will. They are separated by a thin veil, and your cutting into it. Those in the shadows are there for a reason. They are pure evil. They hate god, they hate everything he cares for, and that means above all other things. They hate humanity." The priest paused, "are you there?" She was, she was just in awe, stunned at the random phone call. But quickly grew angry she knew this was something her parents had done to try to get her to quit looking, to quit trying to find the truth

"Fuck off!" She snapped angrily into her phone, before hanging up. It immediately rang. She looked and was not surprised to see the priest calling again, she ignored it, and it began ringing again, he was persistent . she picked it up and screamed "I told you to leave me alone fuck boy!" Hung up the phone again and blocked his number. Things began to get weirder, and her whole life took a turn for the worse after that. The shadowy figures started noticing her more when she seen them, instead of just scurrying away like before they seemed to have a look at her before they disappeared out of sight. She began seeing them in her dreams when she did mange to sleep. One particular night, while she dreamt one of them stepped out of her peripheral and stood face to face. It was terrifying. It looked as if it had been in a bad fire, it had claws instead of fingernails, it's teeth were sharp. It had no eyes, no sockets for eyes, it did have a small pointy nose above it's thin cracked lips. In the blink of an eye it shot a hand out grasped her neck. She gasped, her eyes shot open and she seized so violently she tumbled out of her bed. She was still gasping for air and could still feel his hand around her throat but he was gone.

After she was able to reorient herself she found her phone and decided to make a call to the priest. As she sat alone in her room the only sounds being her wheezing and the ring coming from her phone. Her computer monitor offering limited illumination. Terrified her eyes dart back and forth around the room, seeing the shadows all over hoping that seeing them will cause them to keep their distance. The ringing cuts out just as her vision is flooded with darkness from a thousand shadows.

"Hello? Tiffany hello?" The frantic voice called out through the phone now lying on the floor. "Hello Tiffany? Are you there?"

She wasn't.

-THE OCEAN-

Asia and Raven were quite a pair of young ladies, eighteen and seventeen respectively. They met in college, as they were both somewhat advanced and had managed to skip classes in high school. Being two of the youngest girls in their classes they immediately became drawn to each other. Asia and Raven spent most of their free time together, they studied together, and became the best of friends. Their bond was only strengthened as they began to realize how much they have in common, including their sense of adventure. In the short year and a half that they had known each other they became less like best friends and more like long lost sisters.

After the long semester summer break finally rolled around, and the two girls could not have been more excited. It was decided that they would do some of the crazy things that they've always wanted to do but have never had the chance to do. It's always one of the same three issues that impeded them from going on their grand adventures; no money, no time, or no one to go with. How can you do something death defying without someone going along with you? You have to have someone to help psyche you up for it. And now they both had a partner in each other to provide that support. Raven met Asia at her house, excited as they could be, Asia's mother walked her out, she had been trying all day to convince her daughter not to go, but Asia wasn't having any of it. Her mom warned her that bungee cords could snap and she could be injured, or worse. Asia was still unaffected. While walking to her car to meet Raven who was already in, and buckled her mom pulled her to the side. "Asia, sweetie, you can call it mothers intuition, or just a bad omen, or some kind of telepathy, but I have a really bad feeling about this trip, about your bungee jumping... please don't go." Her mother pleaded with her, but was met with typical teenage apathy as she just rolled her eyes.

"We're gonna be fine mom, we'll be with professionals." She hugged her mom who was still pleading, and got in the car. Her and Raven exchanged looks, that said everything that needed to be said, she started the car, put on Pandora, threw it into reverse, backed out of the drive way and they were off!

The girls arrived and had decided to do a tandem jump. They were strapped in and ready to go. Both of them looked at the body of water below them, it was sparkling blue, and you could almost see the bottom. The sun beamed down on them, and the warmth it provided was like a blanket, the breeze that wandered by keeping it from getting too hot. Both girls still sweating bullets. To be fair it could have been snowing and they would have still been sweating. "this would make a decent grave." Raven thought to herself, she was always slightly more pessimistic than Asia, then at each other. Once again, a single look between the two said more than they had the words to. A deep breath was collectively drawn and they jumped.

They descended quickly and the cord soon became taught and provided resistance to slow them down. The cord continued to stretch and they continued to descend until the line was as tight as it could go. Asia and Raven barely had time to think before the bungee that was keeping them airborne released it's tension with a snap. They were pulled back towards the bridge and then began descending again, this continued for a minute or so as they bounced around before ultimately coming to a stop and being hoisted back up. The adrenaline was more intense than either one could have ever imagined. On the way back to Asia's they were already planning their next stunt. It had to be even more wild! Suddenly as if these surrogate sisters shared one mind, they had a mutual thought, looked at each other an spit out "Sky diving." The last adventure that Raven and Asia are going on before school started was a more low-key one, they decided to wind down with a more relaxing and chill trip. They had decided to go on a scuba diving trip. The boat they were on seemed a little rickety and the captain looked like the typical 'salty old sea dog' their instructor was comfortable with him though so they weren't too worried. They had gone over everything on land and once again when they were out in the ocean. Once they were at the spot where they were going to dive, the girls couldn't help but be taken aback by the beauty. The waves rolling in pushing slightly on the boat, water misting up around it. The sun shining off the blue of the water, dancing across their vision.

Asia fell backwards into the water following the instructor, and Raven followed Asia The world was completely foreign under the water, it was peaceful, and amazing. The wildlife down there, it was like being on an alien planet. And the further they went, the more interesting the animals became. They came to a point when they had to turn on flashlights, as the they were so deep that the sun could no longer penetrate the darkness. The girls did their best to keep sight of one another and their instructor but this became difficult as all they could see of each other was a speck of light.

For a second Asia lost sight of the other two light specks but quickly swam back towards them, relieved when they both reappeared, she swam over to the first one, the instructor. She motioned towards Raven's light. They swam over to find Raven's light, floating, without Raven. The instructor pointed up and began swimming, Asia reluctantly followed. Panicking as she reached the surface the instructor tried to calm her down. "Asia, we need to go back down and try to find her, but I need you to stop panicking."

They went down again, this time Asia ignored the beauty that surrounded her. She was focused on finding Raven. Panic set back in when she saw the cloud of red floating in front of her she knew instantly there was something wrong, something has happened to Raven. Asia whirled around in the water, only to see that the instructor had disappeared. She headed up, Asia broke the surface in tears. To her shock, and dismay she found that the boat, the instructor, the salty old dog, they were all gone. She was alone floating in the middle of the ocean. So many thoughts flew through her mind. Where did they go, why did they leave, and what happened to Raven? How was she going to get back to land, there's no way she could swim that far... she just floated and cried for several minutes until she saw something break the surface a few hundred feet away. It was like nothing she's ever seen, and she immediately realized... her and Raven were merely sacrifices. Her screaming was cut short as she was dragged under water, and into the darkness.

-THE NECKLACE-

What is it about "haunted" or "possessed" objects that just freak us out? Just the term makes us wary of the item, makes us afraid. People will throw away or try to give away extremely valuable things, if they perceive it to be haunted, possessed, or even cursed. We all have that gut reaction to a creepy doll or disfigured heirloom, but the funny thing is though. The less odd the item is the more it seems to scare us when things start happening.

I give you for example, a necklace. A gorgeous gold necklace, and the charm, oh how beautiful the charm was. A rose in full bloom with the most perfect ruby in the center. The light danced off the gold making is shine. And when the light hit the ruby it lit up the most vibrant crimson red. The whole thing was more beautiful than one can imagine. But this beauty was a mask a falsehood that disguised the true evil contained within the necklace.

Our story begins with Mackenzie Well to be fair, the story of the necklace actually goes back many centuries before this but Mackenzie is who were going to talk about. She was an average young woman, born in the early two thousands. Nothing about her was particularly extraordinary, and nothing about her would have suggested that she was about to go through what most of us will never experience, and indeed would not even believe.

Her birth was normal, there were no complications or any incidents, except for one major oddity. When leaving the hospital in Mackenzie mother's property bag their was found a necklace, the most beautiful necklace they had ever seen. Knowing it wasn't theirs they attempted to turn it into lost and found only to be told a man had given the necklace to them, he looked ragged, and exhausted.\ When handing the necklace over he told them that it was a gift to the new baby and left them a letter.

"You don't know me, and we've never met. Who I am is completely unimportant, you will never see or hear from me. The necklace now belongs to your beautiful baby girl. With this gorgeous piece of jewelry comes the peace of mind that she will never be alone and will always be watched over. The burden, is passed."

For obvious reason this letter, along with the mysterious gift, freaked Mackenzie7676 parents out a little bit. Even so they were both unwilling to throw away such a magnificent item, but had no idea what to do with it. Neither one of them felt right about selling it, and her mother did not feel that it was appropriate to wear it. They finally just decided to put it in a drawer and forget about it.

Fast forward through time eighteen uneventful years later and Mackenzie is graduating high school. There's a big event and she wants to look the nicest that she can. She went out and bought a brand new outfit for the occasion. She had the perfect set of earrings. She still felt like she was missing something, this leads her to going through her mother's jewelry until she found that necklace. when asking her mom to borrow it, she was told that she didn't have to borrow it, she owns it. Her mom then told her the whole story.

The event went fine, it went great actually. well it was great, all things considered. There was an injury, a car had flew off the road and through a wall, someone was indeed injured but if Mackenzie had not had a sudden urge to step away, she would have been killed. She couldn't explain it, but something had told her to move, to step away from the wall and move to the other side of the room. This inexplicable feeling saved her life.

The next few days had gone by nothing in particular happened, life was normal. After a week or two though her mother noticed she was still wearing the necklace. She would sleep in it, shower in it, and it was becoming odd. It was downright creepy. But honestly who could blame her? Every where she went she seemed to be protected, people kept getting injured and she walked away without a scratch. Split second changes, simple side steps, hesitations, opting to take the second cab. Instance after instance he life was miraculously spared. No, no one could blame her.

Odd as this was it was made more strange by her erratic behavior. Every time something happened she seemed to become more and more paranoid. Her moods grew dark, her eyes, angry. She became withdrawn, distant. Soon enough the ones she loved began talking.

"Is she talking to the necklace?"

"I think it's time to take it from her" more 'accidents' happened around her more often, they became fatal, and more she withdrew, her erratic behavior seemed to have been giving way to madness.

Her and her little brother were awoken to their mother's screaming, covered in blood! Her husband's blood. His throat had been sliced in the night.

Mackenzie, wrapped her hand around her necklace and mumbled a little prayer. In a confused fit of rage and despair her mother lunged at her screaming and clawing at the necklace, claiming it was evil, she broke free and ran to her room, and locked the door. Unfortunately the door was flimsy and her mom broke it open and lunged again. Mackenzie fell to the floor and attempted to crawl under the bed when her mom grabbed her ankles "Give me the necklace lest your soul be dammed to Hell!" Mackenzie screamed

"Never!" Her voice in unison with that of man's twisted and painful. It was so loud the house shook, she produced a knife from under her bed, as her mom fell against the wall. Still speaking with two voices but very calmly now "Father wanted me too, but I will never allow her to leave."

The police found two bodies in the house, the mother and the father, the two children were never heard from again.

-THE LOTTERY-

Have you ever thought about why the lottery gives you a three digit number and a four digit number each day? Well what else can you think of that has seven digit's that are split into three, then four? That's right, the lottery numbers that come out, they're a phone number. The lottery is a telephone oracle so to speak. Someone who seems to be all knowing.

Whoever is on the end of the line when you call that number knows something that you may need to know. Be warned not every number that comes up is actually for or about you. I can't go into much detail but... Well I'll put it this way, the prophecy on the other end is life changing. I don't mean like a revelation that makes you quit smoking or something trivial like that. I mean something like Bill Gates was rumored to have successfully made this call. He was a college drop out going nowhere, and he just stumbled on a software that happened to lead him into billions of dollars.

In order to do this, in order to get your personal telephone number, you must buy a three digit and a four digit ticket together. It has to be in a store that has a security CCTV system, purchasing it using a debit card to double up on the identity cues couldn't hurt. Basically, without going into too much detail you have to be connected to the numbers in order for the correct phone number to be made available to you. I cannot say for certain if the fortunes are forced by human hands, carried out through paranormal, magic or "psychic" abilities, or if it's truly destined and you're just having the future predicted.

When you first call the phone will be picked up, when it is, it won't seem like anything special maybe a random business maybe a random person. Or even a voice-mail. Say hello, state your name, then say "I'm ready." Sometimes getting the prophecy out of them can be a little difficult and the person on the other end may not seem to be 'all there.' If that's the case, talk to them. Strike up a conversation. It can be about anything, weather, family, current events. Whatever the conversation is about, continue to talk with the person, talk for hours if need be, days even. Never hand off the phone, and never be rude. Do not be pushy, and never question them about your prophecy. If you do any of those things, the person you've been talking too will immediately hang up, and if you try to call them back, the number will be dead. If you continue talking just like you're old friends, after a while the person will just stop mid sentence, (i don't know why they do that) and begin telling you something. Listen very carefully, because it will change your life.

The one thing I need you to understand, and I am definitely not 'allowed' to share this but, I feel I'm responsible for so much pain. This is my small way of trying to earn some kind of redemption. If you make that call, if you get that prophecy, it will not always be changed in a positive way, (your life I mean), you see, while I can't say for certain, lee Oswald, from what I understand was told to be in the depository with a rifle to protect innocent lives. He was told that he would be a hero. He was set up, there have been other instances, more recent, at least 3 people were told to be on the flights that were involved in September eleventh.

I'm bringing all this this out here at great personal risk. I will certainly be killed for it, that's just a fact. That being said, please call the number if you get through follow the instructions. If, while when you are attempting to follow through with your fortune, you see something is amiss, if you sense some sort of déjà vu. if you feel that you or the world around you is somehow unreal, if you see the same faces popping up around you at different places appearing to be different people. You need to run, don't stop. Get in your car, leave town, if you have a family for god sakes abandon them! It sounds harsh but what they will go through when caught.

What I've done to men, women, children. You would call me a monster and I would accept that. what could I say, I was under orders? My life was in danger? I had a family to think about? None of these make what I did ok. None of these things can justify my actions. None of these lessen my guilt in any way.

In order for fortunes to be claimed, others have to pay. I'm not sure how it all works, I don't know why but the telephone oracles, need the energies produced from the victims, for so many things. That's why some die, others suffer in prison. It's only those who realize they are being set up, and run. It's only those who try to get their fortune, to take the ultimate gamble, but don't want to pay the price, that are caught and tortured. So as I said just run, never stay in one particular place for too long and never get close to anyone. The reason for this is that when you're caught they will be captured and taken with you.

I hope that I can either save lives, or at least expose the risk. I hope that I can open eyes, to help understand that it's not a guaranteed win, but indeed the ultimate gamble. I just hope, wish, and pray. Although I do not expect god to forgive what I have done. Even Satan would look away from my sin. I expect nothing and will accept any punishment that is handed to me for my cruel deeds. I can no longer live with the blood that is on my hands. That's the reason I've written this warning. This letter which is as good as a suicide note.

I'm so, so, sorry for all I've done.

-DAMIEN'S JOURNEY-

Close your eyes for a minute if you would, and try to imagine what you picture Hell to look like. Have you got your picture? Good. Now please try to imagine a place that exists beyond Hell. This realm sits beneath the shadows, outside of time and space. It sits outside the laws of physics and reality. This is a place that even the most vile, wicked souls in Hell have never been to. Our story is about one man in particular, Damien, and his journey through this realm.

Damien wasn't exactly a saint, quite the opposite, he was a heathen, he drank, did drugs, cheated. He stole from friends, family, it didn't matter. Damien refused to change and lived his lifestyle until the bitter end when the lifestyle caught up with him in the form of a bullet. He stole from everyone who did any business with him, and drug dealers don't appreciate being ripped off. To say that Damien's soul was 'unclean' is a huge understatement. Damien's souls was as black as soot, and so when it came time, heaven would not save him. Instead demons rose from Hell to drag him back, laughing at his pain, screaming and insulting all the way to his final resting place.

Arriving in Hell, Damien found that nothing was at rest in Satan's realm. Chaos seeded by lunacy, souls crammed packed into bunches, with more coming in. There was no order, only panic, terror, and pain. Endless pitch black void illuminated by the eternal fire. Bodies stacked in piles and used to stoke the flame while they squirm and scream in pain, never actually dying just burning. The stench of burnt flesh filled the caverns, the new souls freshly arrived repulsed but those who have been here made ravenous at the smell of food.

Damien had absolutely no plans of staying in this place. When he looked at where he was, he saw that there was a long line leading up to a desk, behind the desk he saw a few men frantically trying to process the increasing amount of souls coming in. The line was roped off with red velvet, no one dared cross it as the ropes seemed to be the only thing that holds back the demons. They were furious and screaming ready to tear limb from limb, anyone who dared cross it.

Damien stood in this long line of thousands of souls. Everyone was on edge and tempers were explosive. While he waited he planned his escape. His opportunity arose in the form of a huge rumble in line, souls spilled out over the ropes and the demons rushed. He managed to slip away from the confusion and chaos. He quickly began looking for a way out. Coming across what looked like an old set of steel doors, he squeezed through a small opening.

Upon realizing that he had just slipped out of the dark lords Satan's lair Damien began looking around searching for somewhere, anywhere for him to hide he found nothing. The land he stepped into was a vast expanse, the things that Damien saw scared him, but the thought of being discovered scared him more. He knew he had to run because Hell is simply a tomb, that rests in the Echo Side.

So Damien does what Damien did best, Damien ran... He ran and ran and ran. Through this barren wasteland. Passing many, many, trees that have long since died. The sky a hot and bloody red, and Damien ran. He came across figures in the distance, it was a small group of children playing. When he got closer the realization, it was almost too much. These children had no heads, but they played as if nothing was amiss, and Damien ran. Thirsty, tired and legs aching begging for him to stop, burning as if the flames of Hell had caught up to him, and Damien ran. He had nothing left to give, his muscles feeling as if no longer under his control, he stumbled and fell to the ground, willing himself up, and Damien ran. Soon his thighs that had been on fire stopped hurting. He looked at them, and found, to his horror, the muscles were exposed, his flesh was decaying, and the muscles began separating from bone, and Damien ran. Soon the muscles completely ripped off his bones, the decay spread, he let out a scream as he crashed once again to the ground this time, he couldn't get back up, and Damien crawled. Damien crawled a great distance, pulling, dragging himself along the ground. Hand over hand, he continued to make his way forward, away from Hell. He crawled until coming to a man, a man living in the Echo Side.

This was a wicked man, pale white skin, a small slender frame, fiery red eyes, and a long black tongue. Damien paid no attention to the man, but the man paid very close attention to Damien He could smell Damien's pain; this wicked man studied Damien as he crawled up. The man noticed that Damien could not walk; seeing this the wicked man laid himself on top of Damien's back, licked his neck seductively, and whispered some sort of demonic chant into Damien's ear.

He struggled but could not get the man to leave. He had no other options. Damien continued to drag himself along with the man still on his back still chanting. He called out begging for this torture to be over, for anything to take him away. He begged for his old life back, even laying in the streets strung out on drugs in the heart of his ghetto was infinitely better than what he's going through now. The wicked man grew weary of Damien. He removed himself, to Damien's relief, to find other ventures in the Echo Side. Damien crawled for hours, now free from the wicked man. But the journey seemed like years. Dragging himself through the dirt, collapsing from exhaustion and laying in bloody puddles. Everything that Damien saw tortured him on a deep emotional level, each horrid sight he saw, picking away little by little at his sanity. And yet even with everything that has happened and everything he has experienced Damien continued to wish for things to get better. He continued to reassure himself that at least he wasn't in Hell.

As he crawled his arms began to feel a familiar burn, the pain radiated from his shoulders and like before, Damien ignored it and kept moving. Just as with his legs, the flesh on his shoulders began to rip and decay, exposing muscle. Again his muscles had begun separating from the bones. Damien collapsed onto the ground as rodents swarmed. They seemed to come out of no where, and they swarmed around, under, and on top of him. The place was suddenly infested with them. Damien attempted to begin moving again when the rodents began trying to burrow into his flesh but his body had no energy and he fell unconscious.

When Damien awoke he found, to his horror, that the decay had gotten worse. The clouds that hung in the sky were as dark as mighty thunderstorm clouds. Heat seemed to radiate from them. A warm rain fell on his face, it should have been refreshing but it turned his stomach when he realized that it wasn't water falling from the dark hot clouds, it was blood. Damien winced as lightning flashed and lit up the sky, the lightning died and what Damien heard terrified ever more than the lightning or bloody rain. It was screaming! Damien began frantically clawing at the dirt, using all his strength to pull himself forward, he could still hear the screams coming from depths of Hell. Every time a scream pierced through the air, the sky would flicker as if in time with the torture the souls in Hell were experiencing.

Damien's arms soon ripped, torn and fell off his body leaving him rolling and sliding through the blood and over the rodents. Being the selfish man that Damien was, he only cared about himself. And very time that he heard these screams it delighted him knowing that he managed to escape. Soon the screaming brought laughter from deep in his gut. Damien began laughing at the screams harder than he's laughed in a long time, he stopped moving and just laughed and laughed. It was the laughter of a madman. After his laughter subsided he began moving along again still unable to stop himself from chuckling each time he heard the screams.

He soon came across more headless children but paid them no attention. They pointed at him, almost as if laughing at him, and began urinating in front of him creating puddles of piss. Damien still paid no attention. He rolled along with a smile on his face. Damien may have escaped Hell, but the Echo Side most assuredly took his sanity. After all the torture, after everything that he has endured, he finally came across a set of giant glorious fortress gates. Relieved, knowing his journey has come to an end Damien quickly rolled into the gates. In his haste he didn't examine these gates at all, he paid no attention to the sign above them that read "hic omnes ingrediunur specs infringtur" it turns out these red gates were the front doors of Hell...and he never knew it.

-THE LOST SPIRIT-

I was on my way home, it was getting dark and I was a bit scared so I ran. I took a shortcut though the small patch of trees that led to the local park. The woods were always so creepy, so many stories about the things that happen in them. I pushed my legs as hard as they'd go to carry me out of there! I tripped and stumbled into the park, it was empty and the almost set sun, was casting weird shadows, I wasn't sticking around for long. While taking a quick break, trying to catch my breath, I heard something from behind me, something in the woods, I ran again!

I ran like the wind, until I couldn't go any further, although I wasn't in the greatest shape so it was only a few blocks. Now with only a few blocks to go, I came to a stop. As I did I heard a loud screech behind me, when I turned around I was looking into the headlights of a pickup truck. There was no time for me to react it hit me, everything flashed white, then it all went black.

I opened my eyes to the sound of sobbing, somewhere in the distance I heard sirens. My head pounded and my chest was killing me, but I was ok. Some neighbors had come out, hearing the commotion I assume, and they were talking to the sobbing driver. I walked up, and tried to explain that I was ok, nothing a large pizza a two liter wouldn't fix, I think I deserve it for being hit. The driver just ignored me, he continued to sob. In fact it seemed that everyone was ignoring me, I was a little pissed. I was the one who got hit, and some how performed a miracle by only being sore, and here you all give your attention to the asshole who couldn't even watch the dang road!

Very quickly the sirens were on top of us as the first responders jumped out of their vehicles, just seconds later my mom came running, I could hear her screaming. Finally a little attention, I grab my ribs, going to play it up a bit. But they ran right by me, didn't even glance in my direction. My eyes followed them to the truck, curious why they would go there. The driver and I are both over here. When I saw it, my heart sank and everything flashed white again and then black. I hit the asphalt.

I awoke in my bed trying to shake the dream I just had, it was already fading but I remember seeing, seeing myself. I had died, hit by a car...weird. I headed down for breakfast, my mom always has breakfast in the mornings. There was no breakfast, I went to my moms room the door was open and I could see her laying face down. Still sleeping, well I guess it's time to learn how to make breakfast, as I turned away I heard her, almost whimpering. I called out to her, "mom." She sat straight up, she looked startled like she didn't expect me to be home,

"Who's there?" She called out, looking at me, through me.

"Ha ha mom." I replied snarkily. "Can I get breakfast?" She laid back down grabbed a picture of me by her bedside, I heard her whisper

"He was only thirteen, why did you have to take him?" She sounded angry, and betrayed, that's when it hit me. It wasn't a dream was it? I was rundown wasn't I?

So I'm dead, what do I do now? Well I spent the next few days crying and trying to cope with the fact that my life is over. I could only cry for so long though, eventually I pulled myself together. I've been a decent human my thirteen years, believed in god, did my best, I figured Heaven will take me soon. Days passed, then weeks, then months passed. Heaven never came. Maybe I was bad, or worshiped the wrong god. But I never felt Hell's flames either. So I wandered, I wandered into psychic's buildings, what a joke. I spent time at the graveyard hoping to find answers, but came up empty. I wandered through the neighborhood, I watched people. I watched them on computers, TVs, cell phones. I watched them waste their precious gifts of life. I watched them and I got angry!

I continued to wander, I wandered into bathrooms, and watched the girls shower, I watched them get ready. I watched pretty girls for hours, talking on the phones, chatting with their girlfriends. I felt like I could be their shoulder to cry on. I listened to them talk about the boys they like, and the boys that broke their hearts. And I realized I'll never get a chance to know these girls, I cried. I cried and I got angry at God for allowing this, allowing me to die, and for not taking me to Heaven.

As I walked the streets the rain poured, the snow fell and everything froze, summer came and the temperatures went, and yet none of it seemed to bother me. What does have me a little concerned though would be the ravens, those dark black birds. I used to see them scavenging for food and being generally normal birds. But now I only ever see them perched... watching. They watch every move that I make, I don't know what significance they hold, but I know they terrify me.

I've gone home, I've sat with mother, watched her cry. I hoped and begged that she would move on, and she's tried but she's never fully been herself. I talked to her, I've yelled, I've sat there and screamed in her face, she still doesn't notice me. I try to use mirrors and windows to write on them, I've tried so hard to concentrate hoping I can focus my energy to effect things. I've tried to move objects, let my mother know that I'm here, but nothing works. Nothing ever works!

I've grown bitter. the majority of my time now is spent angry. I cant find much to make me smile any more I hate the world that left me behind, everyone continues their pointless activities, wasting time, wasting lives. Time, and a life, things I was robbed of, I despise them for that! I've grown to hate my mother, she caused this! I want them all to suffer, my world grows darker and darker, as my anger still builds.

I've learned though, through my anger, through my bitter hatred, I've learned to control people in a sense. Not possession or anything, but I've learned to whisper to them. It started with mommy dearest. I whispered every night to her, how this was her fault, it was her fault I'm dead! It was late, shouldn't have let me been out that late, she should have come to pick me up. She got depressed. I told her there's nothing she can do to make it right, I told here there's only one option left.

Friends found her in the tub. Empty bottles of painkillers and sleeping pills, wrists slit.

For the first time in as long as I can remember... I smiled but that's not where I'm stopping, next is that kid getting bullied in school, I visit him each night. I tell him what to do. How to end the pain. He gets angry, and it makes me feel good, almost alive again. I fill his head with visions of pain, and death. I tell him which house has what he needs. I prepare him to bring Hell to earth. He awoke this morning I can feel his hatred it's glorious! He's ready, walking to school, with me in his ear the whole time, "None of them are innocent, none of them are innocent, none of them are innocent." He arrives at the school, his smile is as mine, he confidently strolls up to the big double front doors and pulls a rifle from his bag.

-MY TRUE LOVE-

She was perfect! My one true love. I couldn't keep myself from thinking about her all the time. When we were apart I missed her so, when we were together, my heart leapt for joy. I was a timid man, quiet, shy. I would back down from any sort of confrontation, but you know, when I was with her, I felt like a man. I felt like a real man, knowing how timid I was, she never pushed, she never made me prove my manhood, and it's a good thing. I wouldn't have been able to, I would have crumbled. She understood, and I loved her for that.

We would go for walks through the park, holding hands, talking, and laughing. Surrounded by nature. The trees full of luscious greens, swaying gently in the breeze. Birds would sing, and my love would look for them. Animals now and then would scamper out in search of food, she thought they were all so majestic, I adored the way she looked at the world. We were in love.

We'd go on picnics, sit together watching the sun go down, setting the sky ablaze with reds, yellows, and oranges before turning to dark blues, and purples as the light fades all together and the moon shines down on us with the most romantic glow. And oh how we'd talk, we shared our hopes, and dreams, our interests, our darkest secrets, our wildest fantasies.

I would take her out too, I would have shown her the world. I offered to take her around the globe, to buy her anything her heart desired, take her to any restaurant, any party, anywhere. If I didn't have the money to take her, I would have gotten it. I would beg, borrow or steal it if I had too. She always laughed, called me silly, and told me that none of that was necessary. Most nights we'd end up in a little dive bar, the lights almost all blown. Only a few remained and when they flickered in the darkness the shadows would dance and move in sync, just as she and I danced when the band played.

It didn't matter what band was playing, or what they were playing. We danced to our own melody, and sometimes we just sat in the dark, the band playing softly enough in the background and we would just let the time fly by around us. We were no longer shackled by it's constraints, we were unaffected while the people around us were pushed forward through it. I would walk her home as the stars shone down on us, the light was beautiful, but paled in comparison to the light in her eyes, they twinkled so vibrantly they brought shame on the stars in the heavens. The most beautiful works of music, from the likes of Mozart, Bach, and Beethoven, were mere street trash compared when she would speak. The birds in the trees could only admire her song. Her beauty was a work of art that none could compete with, her ivory skin, so soft, and free of blemishes of any kind. Her gorgeous flowing brown hair more perfect than silk. She was beautiful, she was amazing, she was mine.

The more I thought about it, the more I couldn't understand why. My god this woman was an angel among us, why has she chosen me? I began to realize we were never going to work out. Someone better would come along and steal her away from me. They would take away my world. I couldn't let that happen! I knew that I had to make her mine forever.

While walking home from the bar on a particularly cool night, the moon nowhere to be found. I reached into the basket that I kept the picnic in from earlier, and rooted around until my hands gripped it. I was nervous, even as cool as it was I was sweating bullets. My hand gripped it, I felt like it was now or never. I pulled it from the basket, hoping and praying. If everything worked out I would be the happiest man on earth. I called her name, my voice broken. It was more like I squeaked her name out. I drew a deep breath as she turned slowly, I caught a glimpse of those wonderful eyes of hers. They rolled back in her skull as the small pipe in my hand, landed on the side of her head. Her body went limp, and she fell to the pavement.

I quickly picked her up and with the utmost care, I placed her over my shoulder and began walking. It was quite a long journey, one that we had made many times, but never like this. I knew that I couldn't allow myself to get caught. I had to stop every so often when a car would drive by. As I trekked on I thought about all the things I had ever said to her. All the promises that I made, all the moments that we shared. I thought about all the wonderful things that we had talked about. I shifted her off of my shoulders and began carrying her as a husband would carry his wife across the threshold. I looked down at her, still just as incredibly beautiful as ever! I leaned in and pressed my lips against hers. Having my love in my arms, it was an indescribable feeling. It made me feel powerful, alive, like a man. I would never let anyone hurt her. I would never let anyone take her away from me.

I continued my way home when I noticed that her blood had begun dripping on the ground, I had to get her back to my place as quickly as possible. After all I didn't want to lose my baby on the way there. I had such big plans for what we would do when we got home. I'd make her my wife. She would take care of me, and I would take care of her. And oh the naughty acts that we would commit would make the devil blush. Many people would disagree with our relationship, but they can say whatever they want, we were in love. All I need in this life, is her happiness, her love, her. We got to the door and I set her down to unlock it, I swung the door open wide. I scooped my love back up and held her in my arms, I gazed at her perfect face, wiped the blood from her cheek, and swept her inside.

I knew that our fairytale was going to have a happy ever after, and that time was growing close. I took her through the house, down the stairs to the basement, this would be her new home. I knew she'd like it. The room was a little dark and dank, it had one window, but I had to board that shut. There was a light fixture in the middle of the almost empty basement but two of the three bulbs were burnt out. I laid her down on an extremely nice mattress, only the best for my baby. I of course had to shackle her to the wall, I wouldn't have anyone trying to take her away from me.

As I got her settled in she started to wake up and come back to her senses. She was still pretty out of it, her eyes fully glazed over, but the look on her face begged for answers. Where are we, what happened, what did you do. I could see her silently begging for questions, but I knew she needed rest. I retrieved a syringe from my tool box on the other side of the room. I gave her the injection and rubbed her head until the drugs took hold and she slipped back into the unconscious.

Days passed and life had been blissful. It truly was our honey moon phase. I walked down stairs to greet her, and there she was, kneeling by the wall, waiting for me. Hands tied above her drooped head, I think she had fallen asleep. I pulled the thin rod of wood from my toy box, drew back and brought it hard across her cheek. She screamed into the bandanna jammed into her mouth. I knew she loved that pain, she got so much pleasure from it. It was hard for me to give her that but she demanded it, I kept swinging as she kept screaming out in delight. I had even had to raise my hand to her. I hated myself for doing it, but it was what my love wanted, so I was going to give it to her. When she had gotten all she wanted I took what I wanted. By the time I was finished she had tears in her eyes. I knew what she wanted, and I could see her begging for her release. I gave her the shot and emptied the contents into her blood stream. How perfect of a marriage do we have, she fell asleep in my arms.

Heading down stairs to see if my wife has arisen from her nap, she hasn't. I walked over to her, placed her head in my lap, she winced, jerked, and looked at me. "Glad your awake sweetie." The look on her face wasn't the love and admiration that she had been giving me though. It was pain, anger, sadness, hatred, and fear. I wanted us to be in love, I wanted us to live together forever. She reached out and touched me with her fingertips, bloody, and broken. I knew what she was asking of me. I just wanted her to be mine. I wanted to be hers, I wanted our love to be eternal. I could see from the look on her face, that was not going to be the case. I looked up to the heavens, begged for one day to be reunited. I grabbed a large knife from my toy box, cut the bandanna out of her mouth, tears fell from my eyes, she was sobbing uncontrollably, begging to be let go. I said goodbye, and with a swift blow to the head with my pipe, I set her spirit free.

-ANNABELLE AND POLLY-

Annabelle, and Polly oh these two...there's not a lot I can tell you about them, where they came from, what they wanted, how they did what they did, but what I can tell you is that I will never forget those two, they haunt my dreams they terrorize my thoughts and I see their faces in my nightmares. I can never get them out of my head no matter what I do, I see them.

It was about six months back, and my mother received these two in the mail, they are a couple of porcelain dolls. And let me tell you, they were the creepiest damn things that I had ever seen. I told my mom to burn them, I begged her to throw them away, to just get rid of them. She refused to give them up unfortunately, as they reminded her of her mom. Apparently she had owned, and loved, porcelain dolls like these. She wanted them, told me that's how they looked back then. I couldn't wrap my head around how children, even in the old days, would want to have such creepy things. I thought whatever though, I'm an adult with my own house right, so who cares what she keeps in her home.

It didn't take long for things to start going wrong though. My mom got depressed, quickly and severely, in the course of just a month. She stopped eating, she stopped drinking, the began cutting herself off from friends and family. She was wasting away, she would cry herself to sleep, that is when she could sleep. she went from being on of the cheeriest people on earth to being hospitalized for depression, exhaustion, and malnutrition. The doctors found nothing wrong with her physically so she was released, but they put her on medication to keep her eating, and to try to stabilize her mood.

She seemed to get better for a while. She started eating, and sleeping again, and she was able to sleep again. I was relieved, but at the same time the not knowing was eating away at me. Why did she down spiral so quickly like that. The only thing that had changed were the dolls coming into the house. The idea that they were causing her problems was ridiculous though. Even so I asked her about them, I asked who had sent them to her, where they had come from. She wouldn't say. She just told me that she didn't know, that they showed up in the mail with no return address. I couldn't tell if she was lying or telling the truth. I asked her to get rid of them and she refused. I grabbed them, I would get rid of the damn things myself! She lost it, she started bawling then lunged at me, she scratched and slapped me, but I wasn't giving in, I wanted those cursed things out of her house. She quickly escalated to punching, and when she punched me in the face, I lost my temper, I shoved them into her chest and yelled "If you want these damn things you can have them." I stared her in the eyes "But I wont be coming around as long as they're here. With that I walked out of the house, got in my car, and drove home.

It had been quite a while before I heard from her again, she called me randomly one day, to say hi, and apologize for the way that she had treated me, she asked me to come over for dinner. I agreed, then stopped and asked "Do you still have the dolls?" There was silence on the other end. I tried again, "Mom do you still have those dolls?"

"Of course I do sweetie." Her voice was as cheerful and sweet as ever. She seemed like she was acting as if nothing had happened.

"I'm not coming over as long as you have those dolls."

There was silence. Then a click as the phone was hung up on her end. Months went by with no contact.

I don't know exactly the extent of what went on that fateful day but, I received a frantic phone call from my mother, she couldn't contain herself. She told me that she was scared, terrified, that someone is in the house with her, and that she had been home alone.

I jumped in my car and immediately rushed over, weaving through traffic, breaking more than a couple laws on the way there. I flew up into her driveway slammed the car into park, I reached in the back of my car and grabbed a baseball bat, I ran into the house.

Upon entering the place the first thing that I noticed was all the blood. It was everywhere, it was splashed on the walls, covered the floor, it was so overwhelming my knees got weak and I stumbled, almost collapsing. I gained my balance and then immediately tore down the hallway. I was following the blood, as the blood patterns got thicker. That's when I seen it. my father, was laying there, dead. My little brother's and my little sister's bodies laying broken next to him. They were all, bruised torn up, it was sickening. My stomach turned and I began vomiting uncontrollably. There was an ax leaning against the pile of flesh, blood, and bone. I couldn't believe what I was seeing. I couldn't believe that this was true.

My mom appeared in a doorway, I looked up and she just stood there. Unmoving, unaffected by the bodies, unaffected by my presence. She just stood there gun in hand looking, staring blankly. She was not staring at me. Her eyes were locked on one of her dammed dolls. The doll was facing her, almost as if staring back, the other doll was facing, looking at my murdered family.

"Mom," I called out to her. "What in the hell happened here? What's going on?" She continued to stare, "What happened mom? What did you do?!" I was shouting, she jerked quickly noticing my presence my mom looked up at me, and began to sob.

"I'm so sorry son," she began to speak. "Look at what have done, there is no escape, and there is no redemption." She sounded hopeless, I didn't know what she meant. she put the gun in her mouth, there was a loud bang as my world fell black.

I awoke in the hospital, and the first thing I did was leave, I slipped out without anyone noticing. I couldn't remember going to the hospital, the last thing I remember I was still at my mom's house. I stole a car seeing as I didn't have my own. I flew back to her house, I knew that I may wind up in jail for what I was doing today, but I honestly did not care. Those dolls they were all I could focus on, all I could aim my aggression and hate at, I burst through the door and met with several officers, who immediately detained me, I just started screaming my head off about the dolls. I wanted them destroyed. The lead detective (I assume) asked me to calm down and step outside, he wanted to talk to me, I agreed and he followed me out.

Once outside he asked his officers to head back inside and he gave me a second to calm down before asking me about the dolls, about why it took four uniforms to hold me down. I explained the situation fully aware that I sounded like a raving lunatic. He gave me a warm sympathetic smile of understanding, "Well my friend, I don't know who did it, but it seems that you wont have to worry about those dolls anymore." With that he handed me a note he said that he had found it on the counter.

"Don't worry about Annabelle and Polly, I've already mailed them to their next home."

-FACES-

It had been a long night, and I was exhausted, I was desperate for shelter. The sky today was particularly harsh, snow falling, blanketing the ground, in from every break in treetops there was in this endless maze that was a forest. Everywhere I looked, I seen green hidden under white. There were no animals that I could see, I'm sure they had either gone south, like the birds or were hibernating in some cave somewhere. As I grew weaker I felt that death was calling out to me, and had I not been so damn stubborn, I would have answered his call.

After hours of walking I had decided that it was getting too dark, the temperature was dropping. I stopped for the night, I gathered up the necessary supplies and built myself a little area to block the snow and help me stay warm and dry. I built a roaring fire with what was left of my strength. I was sure I would die that night, I was sure that I was already dying, as my body gave out, and I began to welcome that sweet unconscious that would carry me off to the other side. Just before I fully succumbed, I could swear that I heard whispers all around me I couldn't make out what they were saying though. I thought nothing of it, nothing more than my brain exhausted and fried, playing tricks on me. My eyes closed, and my body shivered.

My eyes snapped open, my mind reeling as I struggled to get a grasp on my reality, and then it hit me. It all came flooding back to me, my situation, where I was, what I was doing. By some miracle, I was alive, my fire was still roaring, the crackling and popping was quite soothing, and the heat radiating was warm and comforting. The snow still came from the sky, but the sun was up there, hanging in the back hiding away just behind the clouds that sent down the white death onto the world below them. I got up put out the fire by packing snow upon it and trekked on, hoping to find my way home. Hoping to find my way out of this white and green hell hole that I had managed to get myself lost in.

The daylight was gone in what seemed just a matter of a few minutes, and yet, it felt like I had been walking for forever at the same time. The sun had slowly fallen behind the earth, as I continued walking I gathered supplies for a fire and shelter and prepared for another night here. The absence of the sun left an empty black sky, the moon decided it was shy and would not to show it's face tonight. After the previous night though, I was filled with hope, hope that I can make it through another night, hope that I would be able o find a way out. The darkness grew too thick, and I realized that I would have to stop. I walked for maybe another mile, and that's when I swear I could hear whispering again. Once again I dismissed it as nothing but mere imagination. I settled in for the night and slept once again.

This time I dreamt. They were horrible dreams nightmares. I saw visions of myself, frozen solid. I saw visions of my body bloody and wounded, I saw visions of what looked to be cannibals eating my flesh, and gnawing away at my bones. I woke up cold, freezing, but sweating. This wasn't good the fire had gone out and I was drenched in sweat, it would freeze and I would die out here. I did my best to dry off, and began walking once again.

My heart leapt when my eyes landed on the most beautiful site I'd ever seen in my entire life; it was a cabin! I ran over and examined it, I couldn't tell if it was used or not so I knocked, no answer I knocked louder and called out to anyone who may be inside but still I got no answer so I let myself in. The cabin was just a small thing, built from logs, it had an old time feel but I had a feeling it was more modern, it was probably a hunting cabin that someone had built. This was perfect, I could ride out the storm, I could wait for people, I could be here and get rescued. I settled in the main room with a fire place. How happy I was to see that there was wood!

I started a fire, the light splashed onto the walls, and I huddled in close to it and laid down for a rest. I laid there for hours as the sun went down. When the heat got to be to much for my face I rolled over, and a shiver crept it's way down my back. the person who owned this cabin had questionable taste in decor to say the least. There were paintings all over the back wall. I could hardly make them out at first, but they looked like pictures of people, angry people. The expressions on the faces were big, and exaggerated. They all looked hateful and angry. I hadn't noticed these before, truth be told I don't know how that was even possible. They were starting to make me quite a bit uncomfortable, it felt like they were staring at me, but the alternative was death I couldn't go outside, I couldn't go back to hiking through the woods, hoping to possibly find my way out. I would certainly die out there. There was no question about that, so I decided that the pictures really weren't all that bad and I went to sleep.

I awoke the next morning to sunlight washing over my body, it felt nice, and with the fire still going filling the room with warmth, I could almost forget where I was, almost. "Sunlight?" The word echoed through my brain as my mind raced to attempt to process, something was wrong but my brain couldn't figure out what it was. I whipped around to see the where it was coming from. And to my horror I found no pictures at all, I found that all those twisted angry faces, were gone. All that I found were windows.

My eyes must have playing a trick last night I thought,

that must be it. It was just an illusion due to the night I had had. The exhaustion, hunger, and hopelessness of the situation I had been in, they caused me to hallucinate, I tried to rationalize but, I couldn't convince myself.

I decided that I would check for foot prints but the sky had become angry and the snow was blinding. I couldn't see more than twelve inches in front of me, the wind was whipping harshly. The elements had wiped out any signs of movement outside, even my own.

I knew that I couldn't leave, if I did, the way the storm has kicked up there is no doubt I would die. Knowing this I decided that I was just losing my mind with the faces, they were just windows in the darkness. I was being silly. I decided that it would still be best if I would hold up in this cabin until I was found. The fire started to die down a little bit and I knew it would go out if I didn't do anything. I couldn't let it go out unless I wanted to freeze to death as I began to place more fire wood in the place, I noticed something off, it looked like some dirt had been tracked in to about five feet from where I was laying last night, the dirt scuffs... they were footprints. Leading in from the door.

These footprints, they didn't match mine. Someone was in here with me last night

-LIGHTNING-

We were kids, just kids in the grand scheme of things that is, Ethan was twenty-one and I was twenty-three. What him and I were about to go through on this particular day... I wish we had just stayed home. I wish we could have remained blissfully unaware until the end. That just wasn't meant to be though I guess. We were laughing and having a good time, out in my ford truck out in the middle of nowhere. Ripping through the mud, and just generally tearing shit up. After we were done here we had plans to go out to where we like to shoot and have some good target practice. It was a typical outing for the two of us.

Every thing was normal until the earth shook. It wasn't just an earthquake, it was much stronger. What had me the most off my bearings is that just before the earth shaking there was a single bolt of lighting that fell to the earth. When it struck it felt as if something solid had hit the earth, hard. It was hard enough to shake the earth so bad that my truck actually shook. I stopped driving, and the two of us just waited, neither one of us wanted to admit it but we were scared, really scared, but that was it and everything seemed to be normal after that.

"I think that's enough mudding for today." I looked at Ethan, he gave me a nod in response, as I went to drive away, to my horror the realization set in. I was stuck in the mud. To be fair to my truck's ability, stopping in the middle of a particularly deep spot probably wasn't the best idea I ever had. We got out and after some clever maneuvers we managed to get loose. I drove out and headed for home, he and I decided to go to our shooting spot first though. We were being ridiculous, being scared of a little, or not so little earthquake.

A few miles down the road I noticed something on the left. One of the fields had a long trench, for lack of a better term. Something had crashed down and left a trail. "Probably a meteor" I heard the voice come from the side of me, but I was so lost in thought trying to see the object that I forgot Ethan was still there, it startled me, and I jumped a little. He thought it was funny.

"Yeah it probably is, think we should check it out?" I was going to regardless of what he said but I asked anyways.

"Sure we can go shoot afterward." I turned off the road and followed the trench. I fully expected some kind of smoldering rock. But what we discovered, what lay in the center of the crater left from impact. I couldn't have ever dreamed I'd see such a thing. It wasn't rock, or satellite, or even a spaceship. It was a woman. We were the first to discover her, I looked around, no one was in sight. As I pulled closer I could see that she was beautiful, or at least she had been at point. I got out of my truck and ran over to her, where she lay in the dirt. Lying there she was bruised, a lot of her amazingly silky skin was covered in bruises as if she had been beaten extremely badly. She was scorched, burned all over. I stood frozen, just staring at her. I had no idea what to do. I thought her dead, as she lay motionless. I looked at Ethan as if to ask what we should do, and he shot back a look of pure confusion. He was as clueless and dumbfounded as I was. Who, or I guess a better question is, what is this being that fell from the sky? Was this some kind of experiment by the government to create super soldiers. Ones that could survive some kind of huge impact? I had no idea. I felt it best to simply call the police and let them deal with whatever it was that I was looking at. I pulled out my phone to call nine-one-one, but found that out here I had no reception, I should have known better that to think I would.

I stood there contemplating on what I should do, before finally deciding that it would be best to get help in the closest town, I turned to Ethan to let him know we should go. When I did he had a terrified, and confused expression on his face. "What's going on Ethan?" I asked. He raised his hand and pointed behind me.

"Jeff..." He paused for just a second. "Look." I spun and seen that her chest was now moving, she was breathing. I was as stunned as Ethan but not terrified. The woman stirred slightly, and soon she began coughing. I rushed over to help her in any way that I could. She pushed me away, she got up on one knee, and braced herself, she was weak , and in incredible pain. Once again I tried to help, I thought that maybe stabilize her, but once again she pushed me away. I wanted to do something for her, anything. I wanted to bad to help her but she wouldn't allow it. She looked at me, and just shook her head. I watched as she gathered her strength and willed her legs to work. she stood up, albeit a bit wobbly but she was standing. She was still incredibly beautiful, probably more beautiful than anyone I had ever seen. Once again she looked over at me, and at Ethan Her beauty made my heart happy, but look she gave us, it was so painful, the heartbreak in her eyes, it seemed as if she was begging for something, silently begging, her look was so painful that I almost wept.

"I'm so sorry." The woman spoke and her words drifted like beautiful music, more soothing than any song composed, than any notes put to paper. I fell in love with her right there. Total complete and unconditional love.

"We tried, I tried." She continued, what ever she was talking about I didn't care, it didn't matter to me at all. I loved her! She spoke again. "I have failed you." She gained solid ground readied herself. Then shooting out of her back, two giant wings. She was an angel, but they, like the rest of her body, were scorched and bloody. She gave me one final look filled with sadness and regret, I understood, the begging in her eyes, she was begging for our forgiveness. Then with mighty force her wings extended upwards and then shot down, she was taking off and it was glorious. The angel managed to get about ten feet up into the air before her broken wings could no longer sustain flight and she fell again. I rushed over to catch her. Before today, I didn't even believe in angels. Now I'm running to catch one that cant even fly anymore.

Holding her in my arms it was apparent she was drained of strength, she had nothing left to give and she was dying. The sky began to rumble and the ground to shake as bolt after bolt of bloody red lightning began raining down, crashing into the earth and creating craters as they hit. More and more angels fell from the sky, as far as could see, they like the one before me, were bloody, broken and burned. Again she spoke to me, in that heavenly voice, so full of pain. "I'm so sorry, we, the angels, have failed you." I tried to interrupt and comfort her but she continued. "Go be with your family, this is humanity's end. We fought for you, we fought our hardest even to the point of giving up our eternal lives to try and defend humanity, but, he's too strong, I, we are sorry!"

I couldn't stand it, the pain that she in, the torturous physical pain was nothing compared to the emotional pain she was going though, I felt just a piece of it and began crying. I couldn't compose myself so I continued to weep. Finally through my tears I managed to question her "Who? Who is too strong?" The answer she gave was not what I was expecting. What she told me, well, I knew all hope was lost.

With her final breath she whispered;

"God."

-CLAP CLAP-

One day, a young married couple went hiking in the mountains. They were the adventurous type, but had wandered too from from the normal trails. As the sun began to set, they realized that they were lost. The wife was getting worried, but her husband tried to calm her down and assured her that they would eventually find their way back to their car. However, after walking for hours, they still had no idea where they were. It was growing too dark and too cold for them to stay out, and the man and wife were getting desperate. They didn't have a map or a compass with them and all of the trees looked the same. Just when they were about to give up hope, they came across an old cabin in a clearing.

The cabin looked as if it had seen better days. It was dilapidated and seemed like it hadn't been used in a long time. Some of the windows were cracked and broken and a lot of the tiles had fallen off the roof. As bad of shape that it was in, it was still a godsend to the young couple. The husband knocked on the front door but there was no response. When he turned the handle, it slowly creaked open.

Inside, they found it was in a bad state of disrepair, just as bad as the outside had been. There was very little furniture and the floor was covered in a thick layer of dust. As the couple cautiously looked around, they noticed a strange atmosphere and a peculiar musty smell. The walls were covered from floor to ceiling with graffiti. Written in red paint, the words, "death! Death! Death! Death! Death!" Were repeated over and over again. The man and woman were unnerved. With a shaking hand, the husband reached out to touch the wall. He was horrified to find that the paint was not yet dry. Who ever had painted that, would have had to have done it in the past few hours.

The couple was understandably pretty frightened, but they had nowhere else to go. They knew that the mountain was dangerous at night and there were lots of wild animals prowling the woods. Despite the creepy writing on the walls, they decided to stay the night. Heading upstairs, they found a moth-eaten mattress that was covered in stains. The husband and wife wrapped themselves in an old piece of carpet to keep warm and tried to make themselves as comfortable as possible under the circumstances. They lay down together on the mattress and eventually managed to fall asleep.

Sometime after midnight, the couple were awakened by a strange rustling noise. It sounded like someone or something was moving around outside the shack. "did you hear that?" Asked his wife. "i think there's somebody out there." Her husband listened for a while, but he didn't hear anything. He got out of bed and walked over to the window. It was too dark outside to see anything. Opening the window, he stuck his head out.

"Who's there?" He called nervously. There was no answer. He was about to go back to bed when his wife said,

"Maybe it's someone who can't speak…" That was absurd, he thought to himself but, he wanted to humor his wife, so the husband returned to the window and said,

"Is there anybody out there? Clap once for yes and twice for no." He strained his ears to listen. The stars twinkled in the night sky. The crickets were chirping loudly.

All of a sudden, he heard a loud clap! The man turned to his wife and said in surprise, "you were right. There's someone out there." He leaned out the window and his eyes scanned the darkness. He couldn't make out anything in the pitch black. "are you the owner of this cabin?" He asked.

Clap! Clap!

"Are you a man?"

Clap! Clap!

"You're a woman, then?"

Clap! Clap!

"Are you even fucking human?"

Clap! Clap!

A chill ran down his spine. He swallowed hard and croaked, "Did you come here alone?"

Clap! Clap!

"How many are with you? Clap once for each person..." the response terrified him to the core.

A roar of applause, to rival one following a great performance, erupted from the darkness. The man stood leaning out the window in awe, not sure what to do next. "Do you want to hurt us?" He asked

Clap! Clap!

Do you want to kill us?

Clap! Clap!

"Are..." He hesitated afraid the answer to these questions are lies "Are we safe through the night?" He received silence in return, after several minutes of listening closely he repeated the question

"Are my wife and I safe here tonight?"

Clap! Clap!

"Are you going to hurt us?"

Silence.

Starting to panic he called out "Are you going to kill us?"

Silence.

He leaned back in and telling his wife to start barricading the doors with what little furniture they have, "You said you didn't want to hurt us, or kill us. What do you want from us?" the response he got was worse than the silence. One word pierced the darkness, with a low growl unlike any animal he's heard.

"Feed!" The word feed seemed to set off a chain reaction, all he could hear were low growls erupting out of the darkness,

This was it and he knew it, but he would not die or let his wife die, without a fight! He barricaded the doors, and shoved a mattress out of the window on the top floor, "If those creatures whatever they are get in we're going out" he told his wife as he searched for anything that may work as a weapon. He found a hunting knife, it would have to do,

Not too much time had passed after the growling had subsided he noticed the night was silent. This terrified him. There were no animal sounds, not birds, not even crickets dared to chirp. The man watched as something began approaching the cabin, he couldn't get a good look but it moved on all fours, and it seemed to be smelling the air, once it was satisfied it stood upright

Clap! It echoed in the silence bouncing off trees. Soon the clap was answered back by that minimalistic growl, and the creature responded

Clap! The noise immediately drown out by leaves and sticks crunching and breaking under many of the creatures, the front door flew off it's hinges barely slowing them down, as they flooded into the cabin. "Alright it's time to get you out of here." The man said to his wife, terrified and with tears in her eyes she tried to protest but he was already shoving her, "When you're out, just fucking run, don't look back."

The creatures were already at the door he'd barricaded by the time he turned around, he gripped the knife as the wood started to splinter, that old furniture wont hold up much longer, the man's adrenaline pumped as he prepared to buy his wife as much time as possible, the door cracked in half and was tossed aside. The man got a good look before lunging...

As she ran she could hear the door crack from the cabin, she heard her husband shout, probably attacking the creatures, she ran as fast as she could until she heard her husband again. This time it was a scream of agony, she knew that he had sacrificed himself to save her life... The woman stopped running, smiled and pulled a small map out of her pocket.

Many years had passed since the incident on the mountain in the woods. She stood on the balcony overlooking the acreage that she and her family lived on, she thought about the past, she thought about the future. Looking back into the house, she thought about her family. The man that made her happy, fulfilled her in a way no one ever has. Sure he was well off, but she would have been happy if they were so poor they had to live in a shack, she loved him. The night was getting chilly, but she enjoyed the alone time. Her children we're quite the handful, but she wouldn't trade them for the world

She was entirely and completely happy. Mistakes of the past were long forgotten, and things were good. The woman smiled once again and went to head back into her house. As she did she heard something in the distance, coming from the trees on her property. She hesitated but brushed it off as an animal. She went inside, found her children sleeping in their rooms, kissed each of their foreheads before lying down next to the love of her life. She fell asleep

Once again the woman stood on the balcony, leaning against the railing, glass of wine in hand. Her husband came out to check on her, he was such a sweet loving man, she said she was fine just enjoying a little quiet time, he raised his beer and clinked it against her glass, "Amen to that." he snickered and went back inside.

She had finished off her glass and was contemplating heading back in when she heard the growl of an animal. It was definitely just an animal she thought to herself, definitely just an animal. Then she heard it again, it sounded more human this time. Someone was out there, on her property, trespassing! "Who's out there?" She called into the darkness. The darkness responded with silence. She tried again "Is someone out there?" The response terrified her to her core, she couldn't move, she couldn't even scream.

Clap! One single clap froze her in place, how she wanted to get her husband, to tell him what was happening, what she'd done. To tell him what was going on. She stood there working up the courage to ask another question, maybe this was just a terrible coincidence. "just go away! There's nothing for you here! Just go away and leave me and my family alone ok?!"

Clap! Clap! She knew what this was, she abandoned them so many years ago, she stopped feeding them. She moved away, moved on, and forgot. But they didn't forget about her. "what do you want from me?!" She screamed, prompting her husband to appear in the doorway holding a baseball bat. She broke down crying and the answer that she knew was coming, the answer that she dreaded, cut through the darkness in the form of a rumbling growl "Feed!" She continued to weep as figures began appearing from the shadows, tens of them. As they drew closer to the house the security lights washed over them. Stunning them for a second but it was long enough for her husband to get a good look at them. They looked like humans, or like they used to be humans. They were deformed, they looked wild, there eyes glazed over, they ran and acted like animals he was unsure of what they were. They charged at the house! Some slamming into the walls others through windows and others still splintering the doors as if they were made of particleboard. They were in the house before she or her husband could do anything to stop them. They tore through the house and some made their way to the stairs. Her husband charged down the hallway meeting the sickening creatures half way, determined to stop the from getting to his children. He began fighting but it was useless there were too many, and they were too strong. She stood still frozen in horror watching her beloved be torn limb from limb. She watched as they sank their jagged broken teeth into his flesh ripping out chunks. She began sobbing knowing her children were next and there was nothing she could do.

Her whole family brutally massacred they come rushing up to her but for reasons unknown to her, they don't attack. They stop and wait almost as if something is stopping them, perhaps they recognize her. From behind the group she heard it again "Feed." And she understood the pack would not attack because of the leader. The creature came up to her, behaving like a dog, smelling her, sizing her up. It was huge, almost twice the size of the others. And it wore the scars of fights previously, most likely in this tribe of savages they were fights for dominance. It spoke again, it sounded angry "Betrayed!" And with that jumped on her, and sank it's ragged jaw into her throat.

The door cracked in half and was tossed aside, the man got a good look before lunging, the creatures were disgusting almost human, but at the same time with no shred of humanity in them, they were deformed monsters. He was a strong younger man and fought hard. With the first lunge he swiped and sliced the neck of the first creature through the door, then the second and the third one. He stabbed at the chest of one and when it lurched back, he lost his weapon. Running on adrenaline alone he grabbed the leg of a half of a table he had used to barricade, and swung it. He swung the half table and all, it connected on the side of one of the creatures, and it fell over dead with a broken neck. The table all but disintegrated, but the leg he held was solid. Continued to swing it, connecting with head after head.

He fought for a good hour or two. He killed at least seven or eight of these monsters. He could not keep count. For reasons he didn't know, and was too spent to care, they stopped attacking. He was bitten, bruised, battered, scratched and generally messed up from the fight. His muscles ached, and his vision was cloudy. First they stopped attacking and then started to back toward the ways out of the cabin. He fought it for as long a he could but the blackness crowded his vision and soon he fell unconscious.

When he awoke, his whole body was throbbing. The area around the bite marks had turned black, purple, and green. Streaks lead from his wounds, all leading toward his chest, he wasn't a doctor, but he knew when he was screwed, and he was definitely screwed. Parts of his body swelled and pain radiated from everywhere. He tried to stand up but the pain intensified to a level he could not bare, and he fell unconscious again.

He shot up in his spot to a sitting position and screamed out in pain. Growls and other animalistic noises responded. He looked around and seen the creatures that he had previously fought. He should have been terrified but he wasn't. he sat there in pain trying to think. The thoughts were slow, and hard to come by. He looked down and noticed that the bites were swelled shut. But the trails from them, they led from the wounds, to his heart, but for some reason that didn't kill him. They also branched off, and some went for his head. He wasn't sure, but had an idea that the reason he was having a hard time thinking was because the infection that was going to his brain may have been shutting down higher intelligence. All he really knew was that he was angry, in pain, and hungry. He wanted to feed.

Time had little relevance anymore. He couldn't keep it. He had lost ninety-nine percent of his vocabulary, he lost the higher functioning parts of his brain, he lost most of his memories. He was aggressive, savage, even compared to the other creatures. His body had gone through severe mutilations. One day the biggest creature barked an order and this man, this former man, refused it. the leader and the former man fought. It was a brutal fight. It ended with the leader having an arm ripped off and the former man ripped into it's throat with it's jagged teeth. He was the new leader, the pack accepted this as he tossed the old leaders carcass to them, and they began to devour the mutated flesh.

-THE DISEASE-

The end came quick, in the blink of an eye. So many people changed. The world wasn't ready for it. The military wasn't prepared to protect the unchanged citizens, the center for disease control had no plans in place, there was no cure, no hope of a cure. The disease wiped out a majority of the population, almost overnight. Well, it didn't wipe them out so much as it changed them. It turned people against people, all of the sudden families were being torn apart. The thing is that it was families that were tearing each other apart. This was the real issue. Children began ripping into parents, parents gunning down their children in cold blood. People started acting like animals.

On that first night I remember stumbling out of bed, like I do every morning. My body was weak, not fully awake yet. I was late to work, so I just threw an outfit and headed for the bedroom door. I shambled out into the living room. Apparently my roommate had been watching the news all morning and knew way more about the out break than I did. Apparently it also had him paranoid. When I seen him, I called out and he flew off the couch. Before I could even react, I was staring down the barrel of a shot gun. I fell backwards and grunted out a cuss word at him. He just continued pointing the gun at me."Whatever." I grumbled at him. "I'm going to work." I crawled to my feet and walked out of the house.

In the confusion of having a gun pulled on me, I had forgotten my keys, well work wasn't that far away so instead of going back into the house with that lunatic, I decided that I should just walk. Keep in mind this was before I knew about the outbreak. It didn't take long for me figure out that something was wrong though. Noticed a bunch of people walking to work. Way more than usual. Well little did I know they weren't walking to work, they were fleeing the city. The outbreak had caused people to go nuts.

The first real crazy that I came across, besides my weird roommate that is, was some lunatic with a gun. He was firing into the crowd of us! What the hell?! He was gonna kill someone. I felt like running away, but luckily a few people managed to take him down and wrestle the gun away from him. People were acting so weird. I tried to talk to the guy next to me but he just looked at me like I was stupid and kept walking. "Yeah up yours too buddy!" I muttered.

I arrived at my building to see waves of people rushing out of it. I tried to get someone to talk to me, to explain what was going on, to try to see if anyone was normal at this point, but they all rushed by me. They acted like they didn't even see me. I got bumped into, even pushed. I was knocked to the ground by the wave of people. I was pretty sure that I was going to die when I felt a foot land on my chest. These animals were literally trampling me at this point. This was absolute madness.

Thank god I was able to get back to my feet, fuck this! I'm taking the day off. I decided to head back to my apartment and get my keys I was going to the beach for the day. Well I made it back to my apartment and the door was locked, and barricaded, I called to my roommate, but he didn't respond I was getting frustrated and headed over to look into the window, and sonuva... someone broke my window! I started to get a little worried, were people looting? I didn't think so, I didn't have anything to steal. No I figured in the confusion someone just threw a brick or something. I stepped over broken glass walking up. I crawled in through the window, my roommate was long gone it would seem. I grabbed my keys, unblocked the front door, and left. I climbed into my car, put the keys in and started it up.

I was beginning to get hungry, although it wasn't surprising, I hadn't eaten all day. I figured I'd grab something on the way out of town. I was parked on the street, so I threw it in drive, as I stepped on the pedal another psycho came roaring down the road and opened fire on my car! I couldn't tell if he was trying to kill me, or just scare the shit out of me, he definitely succeeded with the latter. I pressed the gas again, a little harder than I meant to. My tires squealed and my car lurched forward, I tore down the street. I felt woozy, maybe from the adrenaline spike and then wearing off, maybe it was because of the sudden movement, maybe it was because hadn't eaten. Suddenly I felt dizzy, as if the car was spinning. Imagine my surprise when I realized, it was. Someone hit my car and sent it into a spin. What the hell did that disease do to people. My car came to a stop when the ass slammed into a tree, I jerked hard, opened the door and spewed my guts out.

My car had stalled, when I got back in, it wouldn't start back up. I decided it was best to just get out and walk. There was a group of people fleeing the city, and to be honest I couldn't blame them, as a matter of fact I had decided to join them. I could hear gunshots and screams echo from the city I was trying so desperately to get away from. So I looked at the group of people walking by, and shuffled a little faster to catch up. I wasn't sure where they were going, most of them were pretty scared for their lives. The general feel of the crowd was definitely fear. No one really understood what was making people act like animals, why they wanted to kill us, why they were losing their minds. We had no idea what the disease had done to them.

We walked to the next town, hoping to find some safety, and some food. As our group of refugees for lack of a better term, approached the city, we were met with the same treatment that caused us to flee the other city. People were firing wildly into us, they hit a few people. One day and people were devolving. Whatever had broken out it was turning people into violent wild monsters! We turned tail and got the hell out of there, we lost a few people but gained a few as well. A few people that weren't absolutely nuts-o. We walked for hours. On the empty highway, cars had been abandoned. The traffic had gotten too congested and I guess people just got out and walked.

We finally came to a town that was abandoned. Thank god there were no crazies here, no one shooting at us, or trying to murder us. We split up looking for supplies. I could feel myself getting weaker, I was so hungry. I stepped into a house and when I seen him, I knew I was dead. One of the crazies. He was holding a gun, pointing it at my head. He was screaming but I couldn't really here what he was saying, I was too focused on the gun he had trained between my eyes. He pulled the trigger, and I winced expecting death, but the gun just clicked. He was out of bullets! I was so relieved. He fell back against the wall, crying. Is this the next symptom of the disease

Hunger washed over me, uncontrollable hunger. All at once I had a sickening thought. One that disgusted me, but I couldn't resist. I reached out with a throbbing arm toward the young man that almost shot me, and I got a glimpse of it. a huge hunk had been taken out of my arm. A bite mark with black streaks running up it. I didn't have long to think about it, before the ravenous hunger took over. I grabbed the guy.

So hungry.

His flesh looked so tasty...

Just one bite!

-THE BEGINNING-

People always say that death is final, and that's why it's so scary. Even if you do happen to believe in the afterlife once you die, your position in this world is solidified. And the destination for the afterlife, whichever way you're going, heaven or Hell. Your destination is set. You can no longer make any changes. Everything is final. And finality terrifies people. I am terrified of death.

I'm not scared of death because of it's finality. I'm not scared of where I'm going as a matter of fact. I know where I'm going. Well, that is, I knew where I was going. Now though, I'm not so sure if I know anymore. See the thing is I am, I was sixteen. I had just gotten my drivers license and my parents had bought be a new car. It was a used car. But it was new to me and I loved it! It was a small four door sedan, bright red. It really wasn't anything special as far as cars go. But what it symbolized, was amazing. I now had freedom, and I had the trust of my parents. I could do anything, I could go anywhere! I was a free woman... when mom and dad said so.

Mom and dad had, of course, given me a few rules that I was to follow. Like any good parents would, but unfortunately me being a teenager, I thought I knew everything. I was invincible, all the bad things I see in commercials, all the warnings. I didn't think they applied to me, I wasn't as dumb as the stupid examples of teens on TV and in movies. I knew what I was doing. Sure I could check that notification on my phone, probably just I text, I wasn't going to be staring at it, just a quick glance, I wasn't even going to respond to it. Nothing could happen.

Oh god I was so wrong. In an instant, in just a split second while I was looking at my phone I began to swerve into the next lane, to my left. the blaring horn startled me, my eyes snapped back to the road, and I tried to correct my steering. I over corrected and accidentally veered hard into the lane on the other side. I side swiped that car, the collision sent me back the other way, into the first car that I almost hit. at this point I had absolutely no control over my car. I hit that car, bounced off it and while trying to straighten out my car, the back of it began to come forward. My car began to spin. I'm a little fuzzy on the details going forward, but at some point shortly after I had gone sideways my car left the ground. My wheels were pointed at the sky, my head at the ground. It was too late for me to do anything. I couldn't think, I couldn't breathe. Everything happened so fast, but at the same time so slow. I didn't even have time to pray before I hit the ground.

When I awoke I was in an ambulance, speeding away from the wreck. Something was off though, when I opened my eyes and looked around I wasn't on the stretcher. That is I wasn't looking through the eyes of the person on the stretcher. I was more in the corner and I could see the paramedics working on a body. As one of them turned away I got a clear view, they were working on… me, trying to stabilize me. I could see that my body was broken, there was no way I was going to survive the injuries, I knew it. I don't know how I could have been so certain, but I was. I should have been terrified, but, I wasn't. strangely enough, I was at peace. I felt ok, I felt like things were going to be alright. The paramedics did not give up on my body easily but I was declared dead on arrival. This should have devastated me, I was dead. But still I was strangely at peace.

As cliche as this is, I seen the light. It seemed to call out to me, not out loud but, more like within my hear I could feel it asking me to cross over. But I wasn't ready just yet. I looked forward to going, and I believed that paradise was waiting for me on the other side. But I wanted the chance to look over my family for a bit before I left. After all mom and dad had just brought my second baby brother into this world. They spread the kids out pretty good, I was sixteen, the middle brother; 7 and the youngest; just a few months old.

I watched as they got the news. I watched as mom crumbled, she fell to pieces instantly, crying, screaming, cursing, dad stayed strong for her, he held her close while she cried into his shoulder and pounded on his chest. He was devastated on the inside, but he had to be strong for mom. They told Zachary that I had gone to a special place called heaven and that I probably wouldn't come back. He cried because he would miss me, but took some solace in that one day he would see me again. That eased his broken heart, but did nothing for my parents.

I watched dad attempt to stay strong for mom, he never broke down in front of her, never showed how much he hurt. He had always been her rock, and I think over the years, he had forgotten how to show emotion. Even when he was alone, I expected him to lose it but, he didn't. he would sit down in his office, put his face into his hands. And a single tear would fall. Then he grabbed the bottle of liquor he kept in his office. *It was the good stuff.* I had heard him call it that before when meeting for business. Dad really dove into the drinking, any time mom wasn't screaming at him or blaming him for every little problem in her life since the accident. I know deep down she was blaming him for the accident, it was his idea to get me a car. But instead of saying it, she just blamed all her other problems on him. I wish I could have told her not to blame dad though, it was my own fault.

After dad went through all of his *good stuff* he began buying the cheaper bottles, as money was becoming more scarce. He was becoming too drunk to even do his job, and he was spending large amounts of money on booze. This only fueled mom's anger at him. I wish so bad that I could have intervened. On one year anniversary of my death, dad locked himself in his office, and began drinking. He drank bottle after bottle until he fell over black out drunk. On the way down his head made contact with the corner of his desk, there was a sickening crack, he hit the floor and remained motionless. He was dead. I didn't know what to expect then, was he going to show up on this side of existence? Would I be able to see him, or talk to him? Maybe I can tell him it wasn't his fault. But he never came to me. I pray that he made it into the light.

Mom discovered her husband two days later. She realized that she hadn't screamed at him for anything in the past day, when she couldn't find him, she came to the locked office. She had to call the police to come out and break down the office door. She saw him lying there, in a pool of his own blood. He left her all alone to deal with this life. She once again lost it. How could a woman be expected to recover from losing her daughter and now her husband. But she attempted to do her best, she picked herself up and tried to be strong. After all she still had two children to look after. As strong as she tried to be, she just wasn't strong enough. The anger over the loss became too much to bare and she began shutting down. Everything inside her died except for that anger, and her two young boys unfortunately became the recipients of that anger. At first it was verbal abuse, mother got to a point where everything was screamed at the children, it did not take long for that to devolve into physical abuse. Zachary took the brunt of it to protect the baby. Mother spiraled into oblivion in the matter of a couple of months. Zachary, and i, would wince when mother raised her hand. We both knew the back of it would land on his face, the gem in her wedding ring cutting him and leaving a stripe of blood. He had many stripes on his face.

The night all that ended came about suddenly. While Zachary was giving his young brother a bath when he started crying loudly. Zachary did everything he could to calm the young child but it was too late, he had woken mother who was stomping down the hall, already screaming in a rage. She threw the door of the bathroom opened and cursed at both of the children. This frightened the young child and caused him to cry even louder. Mother asked Zachary to leave, he refused afraid she'd hurt the baby. This lead to another back hand, and when the child didn't back down, she doubled her fist in a fit of rage and punched him. He fell backwards out the door. She locked it. Zachary pounded on the door for a short time before running out of the house to get help. I watched terrified and helpless at the events unfolding in front of me.

Mother took the baby out of the shallow water and began rocking him. She seemed as if she had calmed down but she was still shaking. The baby continued to cry and she tried whispering comforting nothings into the babies ear. The baby continued to cry. All at once mother stopped shaking, she stopped whispering, she stopped rocking. She didn't seem angry, she didn't seem to be feeling anything. She set the baby back into the tub and sat on the toilet seat while he cried. She lit up a cigarette and about half way through smoking she slowly rose to her feet, and put the cigarette out in the sink.

She then looked up at the heavens, and began to speak the intense calmness scared me the most "You did this! You took my family away from me. You couldn't let us be happy." she looked at the baby "There's only one way to make our family whole again." She grabbed the young, screaming child by the back of his head and shoved him face first into the water. He kicked and thrashed but she easily overpowered him, and held him down. "Shh," she whispered. "You're going to see daddy, and Katie, and soon mommy and Zachary will be there too." She held him under until the bubbles stopped. She sat there for a few minutes admiring her work. The police came crashing into the house, put her in cuffs, took her to jail. She ended up in a facility for the criminally insane. My baby brother was dead. Zachary should have been so lucky. Little Zachary was taken by the state, and put into the foster care. we really didn't have any family members that could take him, so he was sent to a foster home. Being at the age he was, and his tough exterior due the past couple of years, him getting a home seemed to be a miracle. But somehow it actually happened. I hoped that I could find the light and go into it now that I was relieved that at least one of us was going to finally have a decent life. That was until the man who adopted Zachary started shooting his *special videos.*

-VOYAGER 347-

The world was dying, the earth was running low on resources we had maybe five hundred to six hundred years before we reached catastrophically low levels of them. Fossil fuel was all but gone. The same was true for natural gas. Our freshwater lakes had stated drying up. Humanity had wiped out the forests for cities, it was called progress, what it really was, was our eventual killing of the planet. We didn't think about it at first. When we were demolishing natural resource and natural resource.

We as scientists eventually started running simulations, trying to determine what would happen if we continued the way we were, and the outcomes were dire. We attempted to tell everyone, I attempted to tell everyone. The problem is that we were going up against big business, against billionaires. These billionaires did not want to give up their fortunes, no mater what the cost to the environment. They campaigned against and ultimately snuffed out our messages to the world.

There was no way that we could stop the destruction, so we did the only thing our brilliant minds could think of. We created interstellar ships, the likes of which only seen in science fiction movies. The function of these ships? Look for habitable worlds that could sustain human life. We would need to find a suitable replacement. Somewhere humanity could start over when earth was destroyed.

It took us most of our lives, seventy five years to design and build these ships. I wasn't sure if I would live to see the day that they come back. I wasn't sure if I live to make it to a new world. But I hoped against all hope that I could live that long. A human life span had grown, but it was only around a hundred and fifty years at this point and I had started the process of working on this ship at twenty-five.

I could not have been more proud of my life's accomplishments on that day when we were ready to launch. We had five ships all together five ships would allow us to explore different sections of our galaxy increasing our chances of finding a replacement planet. The launches were flawless, everything went off without a hitch. It took the ships about a year for them to reach the outer edges of the solar system, once there, they were able to drop into hyper space. We waited impatiently for response. When we got it, the news was good, and tragic at the same time. Four of the ships launched sent word to us. The fifth one , we never heard from again. The remaining four had found solar systems. And scanned for habitable planets. None found anything that could be inhabited without significant work. Work that we may not be able to afford.

Back in the command center the cheers and applause roared when we finally got the message. The most wonderful message that we could have received. "we have finally found the perfect planet. It has forests, huge land masses giant lakes of fresh water. The atmosphere appears to be breathable, we are going to check it out." With bated breath the lot of us fell silent and waited for any further word. This could be the answer we've been hoping for, this could mean the survival of the human race as we know it. So we waited. Minutes turned into hours and hours into days. A month had passed. Hope of hearing from them was slim but not abandoned. In a solemn command center, suddenly a voice ripped through the silence. "Hey command, are you there? Do you copy?" We responded and let them know we copied. "The planet is indeed habitable, the air is breathable, it's amazing, it can definitely support our life. The only issue we seem to have is that the atmosphere seems to block our transmissions." We understood, they had collected samples of everything we would need to test.

"We're returning home ask we speak command. Let's have a toast. Here's to earth, here's to the new earth!" This was the last radio contact the world ever heard from voyage 347. It dropped into hyperspace on it's way home.

It has been 10 years since the shuttle had gone dark. Humanity had lost hope, hope in finding the missing astronauts, hope in finding a new world, a better world for mankind. And still the business crushed our message. It wouldn't be long before we pass that point that we would not be able to come back from, that is if we hadn't already passed it. I knew that I wouldn't live to see another ship make it to a habitable planet. I would die on this miserable earth. I only hoped that the people of earth would continue trying to find a better world.

That was until December fifteenth, when NASA finally picked up a signal. It was faint, and broken, but it filled us with just a small glimmer of hope, we put the best people we could on unscrambling and telling us what the message said. They thought it, at first to be unreadable. We didn't have much time to work on it before the shuttle, the one that we lost all those years ago, blipped into our solar system. it wasn't traveling through hyperspace though. It seemed to be drifting. The engines, we observed, kicked on to keep it from crashing into anything but other than that it was adrift. Something was terribly wrong as that was a protocol set in case of extremely low fuel.

We watched as it maneuvered our system, we watched as it passed the asteroid belt, then passed mars, Venus, our moon. We watched, and prayed that it didn't burn, as it passed into our atmosphere. And finally it came crashing right down right at NASA's front door.

We had top engineers and paramedics already standing by for the landing. They were set to do anything that needed to be done to save any crew left, and salvage any of the ship that may still be in tact. We had computer geniuses waiting to retrieve any info they could off of the databases. It was clear that the shuttle had sent that message, but it was just too damaged for us to get it. I had to wonder why they would send a message with the shuttle following so close to it. I tried to shake the feeling. The ship came alive as did myself and all the crew that had worked on this mission, we could not have been more excited. The doors slowly began to open. We were all ready to do our jobs. Hope for a new life, hope for the survival of humanity had been restored. When the door opened I watched in horror as something, something that used to be the captain of this vessel came tearing out of the darkness towards the closest person to him, a doctor. He grabbed the doctor an tore into him, he began ripping him apart. The rest of the crew came pouring our and acted in a similar fashion. They were violent, unstable, they looked like mindless killing machines, emotionless sans rage. Luckily we had armed security, members of our fine military, waiting with us. They dispatched these animals rather quickly. My heart hurt. I had known these people personally before this mission.

Most of them did not have family and that was a big part of the decision to send them, there would be no hard phone calls, that didn't do much to help my pain. Once again I felt that overwhelming hopelessness. I wasn't sure who would take my place when I passed away, who would drive the mission to save humanity. I sat in my office, I had the pistol, that usually sat in my drawer, sitting on my desk. A glass of whiskey in hand, on my computer all the files that someone would need to pick up where I left off. And a note explaining everything. Just as I was working up the courage to finally do what I had planned I got a phone call. The message had been decrypted. He played the audio and ice crawled through my veins. "The crew, they've been taken over by some thing. I don't what it is, some kind of disease or parasite. All I know it that it's airborne, and it's highly contagious. They're violent, primitive, I'm the only one left in his right mind...but I'm fading fast. I can feel the rage boiling inside me. I can feel the want, the need to commit atrocities. I want to tear them limb from limb. I want to spread the blood of my best friends, I wont be able to fight this much longer. Listen if we ever make it back, if this ship gets within range of getting back to earth, please for the love of god, shoot us down. Blow us out of the sky. This is why that perfect planet had no life on it. Please don't let us reach the surface, and above all! Do not approach the shuttle. The fate of the human race depends on it."

I was angry, I cant believe we were this stupid, blinded by false hope. I was red with rage. Humanity was doomed. I took the drink and picked up the pistol.

-THE STARS-

I was alone in my apartment mindlessly watching the news playing some stupid game on my tablet, I don't even remember what it was anymore. The heater was on and it had gotten a little stuffy, and to be honest I was bored with my game. The news was on so I didn't feel as lonely. I know it's stupid but hearing someone talking in the background makes it feel like there are other people around. Deciding that I need fresh air I put the tablet down and opened the window. I peered out, and up at the sky, the stars are always so beautiful, and hey I had gotten lucky.

The weatherman was right for once, there wasn't a cloud in the sky, and while you'd think that I should be happy about this, I really wasn't. something was terribly wrong. The stars, beautiful glimmering specks dancing in the night sky, they were gone. I scanned the heavens and found nothing. Nothing but the lonely moon hanging in the blackness remained. I ran outside and still found nothing. There were no clouds to block their light, and I've looked at them each night, so I know they were supposed to be visible!

At first this was actually quite interesting but slowly it became much more than interesting or even disturbing. this was downright terrifying. What could do this? What could make the light from the stars disappear? My mind raced for possibilities, and came up with nothing plausible. I tried to tell myself the city is just too bright, it wasn't. That there may have been some planes blocking the sky, they wouldn't have blacked out the entire sky. It wasn't long before the whole neighborhood was out in the street everyone had an opinion, an explanation a reason for the occurrence.

No one could have predicted, or even dreamt in their worse nightmare what happened next. Whilst looking up, trying to come up with an explanation and bickering amongst neighbors, we seen it. A giant shadow was cast on the moon, passing over it, as if something large had passed between the sun and the moon. Suddenly the light from our moon, the closest body to earth and the last of the heavenly bodies to still be shining in the sky blinked out. we were shrouded in a thick blackness, with only the lights of our houses, street lamps, and telephones cutting through it. Panic began to spread all at once.

Before we really had a chance to get a group panic up and running, something hit us. The ground shook, the houses shook, everything shook. In an instant, in less than a blink of an eye the lights that we were all relying on, the houselights, the streetlights they all cut out. Our phones shutdown, flashlights immediately stopped working, we were in total blackness. Total isolation with no speck of light to be seen.

Then came the worst of it. That's when the screaming started. It was not screams of terror no one really knew what it was, what they should be terrified of. They were screams of pain, I ran. I couldn't see where I was going, my only form of navigation was away from the screaming, I ran until my legs couldn't carry me any more and my body couldn't handle slamming into anything else. Ran into houses, cars, trees, I tripped over curbs, anything lying on the ground. I'm not proud but I ran into, tripped over, and even stepped on other people. But I continued to run. I ran until I collapsed and passed out.

I awoke to the sun shining down on my face, groggy I

sat up. That was a weird dream I thought. It wasn't dream though, I soon realized this. I was in a strange place that I didn't recognize, it smelled of old machinery and old books. Looking around and examining I found myself to had somehow would up in an abandoned warehouse. I was alone, with the warmth of the sun flowing in through a set of broken jagged windows. I stood up, and instantly regretted it as I dropped straight back to the ground, I was in incredible pain. Slowly I made my way back to my feet and to the open door that I assume I came through.

The streets were filled with blood, and littered with body parts torn limb from limb. Arms, legs, heads, torsos and random pieces everywhere. I was reminded of a zombie apocalypse the way random parts were just discarded. Just taking in the image of what I believed to be complete destruction, I questioned if I wanted to live anymore. I questioned if I wanted to remain the last human on this planet left alive. That's when I heard the voice of a child call out, she was clearly terrified, but so was i, who could blame anyone at this point. I went slowly over to her, introduced myself, and promised I'd look after her until we found her parents. We never did.

I wasn't alone. Millions were killed that night. Dismembered, discarded, slaughtered. I thought it to be the end of the world, but millions survived. No one has any clue what happened, what did this, we all just did our best to move on, and rebuild. And we did. The phenomenon reached across the globe, and the politicians did what politicians do. They argued. The military was beefed up, and the government released a statement that boiled down to; "We don't know what happened but we'll be ready if it happens again." Typical government statement, meaningless but it makes people feel better. Our society is thriving again, we were scared at first but things are getting back to normal.

That was five years ago, and I still watch the sky every night with my adopted daughter we go over every constellation and look at all the stars that we can find. We count them until she begins to nod off. It started off as a way to be vigilant to keep watch. As time went by though it became more of a ritual, a habit like a bedtime story. Tonight is no exception and it's a beautiful cloudless night, the moon hangs in the sky bright as ever. I'm happy. It's a good night, she starts without me, as I make us some hot cocoa with little marshmallows like she likes. I could hear her naming off the constellations as I pick up both mugs. My hands become weak and they crash to the floor when my adopted daughter said something that terrified me on a primal level.

"Where did the big dipper go mom... it's gone."

-SOMETIMES-

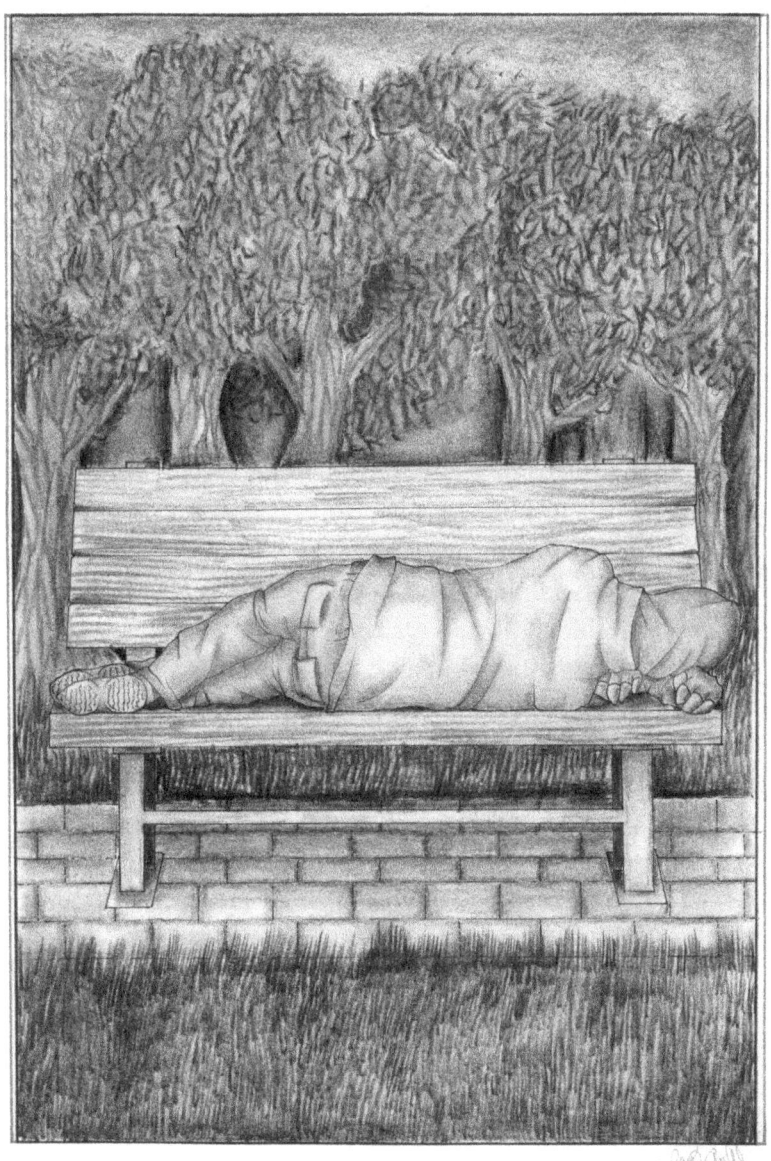

It was a dark and cloudy night, the moon, barely poking through, was casting shadows all around me as if ghosts dancing without the knowledge that they have passed, maybe that's how the story will be told. But in all honesty it was a warm summer night, there was a moon but it was almost full, nothing creepy about it, beautiful, but not creepy. The night was so nice in fact I had decided on a stroll.

God damn that warm moonlit night! I met a young man attempting to sleep on a park bench, normally I would have just walked by, it was uncomfortable sure but as I said it was warm. Something, being a man of faith, I thought the holy father was urging me to talk to the man. He clearly wasn't getting any sleep anyways might just keep him company.

The minutes went by and somewhere along the lines, they turned into hours. Before I knew it the sun was coming up, and dammit all I have work! I wished the man a good day and went to hurry off, as I stood up to walk away he grabbed my arm, "You're in incredible danger...your family is in incredible danger. Death is always watching...always waiting."

It threw me, sure, but I shook it off the guy must be crazy. Just then images flashed in my mind, my wife, my kids brutally murdered, murdered because I wasn't there to protect them! All I could think about as I charged home is what that bum had done to my family or what his *friends* did, I could only think about what I would do to that bum!

I got home, busted through the door barely opened it before I went through it. I went to my oldest daughters room first, as it was the closest...it was locked. I Didn't stop, I ran right through it only to see my precious baby girl jump out of bed in mortal terror due to the rampaging idiot who just busted through her door. I checked on the other girls and my wife, everyone was fine! I went to work and the whole day I felt like a fool.

Upon entering the house coming home from work I immediately took a nap, it was another warm night so I took another stroll, how foolish I had been today, and that's when I seen him. The man I had spent the previous night talking to, I wanted to avoid him, to avoid another all-nighter, but he wasn't tossing and turning on the bench he was just laying there, I thought he was dead, and I remembered all the bad things I had thought about him, and it broke my heart a little. That is until he began snoring. And a part of me was quite relieved.

I chuckled, because that's all I could do, once again I felt like a complete fool. I don't understand it, but he must be a light sleeper though because he stirred I turned around planning to briskly walk away when I heard him call out to me. I stopped, stood frozen for a quick second, then went over and greeted him, but warned that I could only stay a minute. Well we got to chatting and before I knew it (again) the sun came up, as I went to leave he stopped me again. "Your family is in incredible danger! He is watching, he is waiting!"

Not falling for it this time I went home got changed and went to work, came home, no one was there, work, and after-school activities means a quiet house for me to sleep,

This same cycle went on for about a week, damn thing is I couldn't seem to be able to keep myself away, from the park to save my life, I don't know why. It was as if I was drawn to that place, to that man. I didn't know why at the time.

Well one night I was at the park, and it seemed unseasonably cold. I Can't explain it but it was almost freezing. Being the kind of person I am I grew to care about this guy, other than his odd warnings when I go to leave he's been great company, all night for about six nights, I knew almost everything there is to know about a person. And I just chocked his warnings up to his way of saying he's lonely. No-one else pays attention to him they act like he's not a human being so I don't blame him for being a little weird or awkward, when what he really wants is for me to stay and talk.

I offered him a warm place to stay for the night, he had to leave with me in the morning but he could sleep on our hide-a-bed couch. It wasn't all that big of a deal, to allow him to do it. He immediately refused. I pushed the issue, asked him to do it as a favor. Nothing seemed to convince him, he protested saying it wasn't that cold. Then he began to ask me to stay and chat, to this, I had to refuse. I went home, got in bed and was out almost immediately.

When I awoke I found that I was covered in blood, there was blood everywhere! I bolted out and into each of my children's rooms my children were dead, my wife dead. I Called the police and just laid down and cried! When the police arrived they came through door guns ready, they spotted me lying there in the living room bloody and sobbing and arrested me. I pleaded with them I swore I was innocent, I told them about the homeless guy, I swore I had nothing to do with the murders, they didn't believe me. I begged for them to search for the bum, I told them to arrest me but search the house, they did their search, and came up empty. The house was still locked from the inside the only forced entry was theirs. That didn't make sense they don't know how to do their jobs!

Days passed while I sat in a jail cell, I wept. All day I wept, that's all I could do my family, my family was murdered...slaughtered is more like it. The man who did it, he got away and me, well they're going to put me away for a crime I didn't commit. I think the death penalty would be best, the pain is just too much, so I continued to weep. They finally took me into one of those little rooms and asked me to tell them my story, so I started from the beginning.

They listened to and recorded every word they seemed interested but they didn't believe me. One of the *fine* officers showed me pictures. I wept as they showed me that the marks on my wife's neck, seemed to match my hand, they showed proof it was my fingerprints on the knife used to cut my daughter open as if performing a crude autopsy, the bruises on my youngest...the ones that remained after she had been savagely beaten to death...they perfectly matched my fists! I wept uncontrollably! I swore the man in the park had drugged me or something! Somehow he was responsible...that's when they produced the security tape they had gotten a hold of, turns out the vandalism and crime in the park made them put cameras up a few years back, than god for those cameras!

My heart skipped a beat and for one split second through my tears I felt a small amount of joy! They can see the bastard, and track him down. I bet he'd fold under a little bit of pressure. What I saw on the tape it was so unreal. It wasn't possible.

It was just me, there was no homeless man. I was sitting on the bench...talking to nothing, They fast forwarded through the week's worth of tapes...the man sitting there keeping me from going home, warning me of danger that waited for my family. The doctors say that it was just my psyche splitting. They said that part of my brain knew what my intentions were so I created a persona to keep me away. A hallucination that stopped me from going home, that kept me away from my family to keep them safe. They said that part of me had a growing resentment and anger issues. but I don't believe that though. I was not an angry person. I loved my family more that life itself. What I believe is that I was in the middle of a war. A demon possession, versus an angel attempting to save me, my family, and my immortal soul. Unfortunately for everyone involved though, this isn't some movie where everything works out. Sometimes...

Evil wins!

-A SECOND CHANCE-

The day had come. I sat alone in my house. I waited quietly in the dark. It was time again, how many times would this have to happen, how many time had it happened? I sighed a deep heavy sigh. I knew that soon enough he would be stepping through that door. I knew why he was coming and I don't think I'd ever really get used to him. I knew soon enough someone new was going to have to die.

Was it worth it? hell I don't know anymore. I felt like it was at the start, but looking back, I don't if it was ever worth the pain caused. Could I stop? Never. It's never gotten easier, although I hate myself each time. More and more I hate myself for what I do. But, yet I don't dare stop. Years must have gone by, no, it started decades ago I suppose.

I was a timid man, sure I've done some wrong in my life nothing too bad, nothing up until the day that, well the day that everything kind of fell to shit. I could hear someone screaming for help a young girl being attacked, but what could I do? In this big city I'm sure someone would help that girl, someone would call the cops and intervene. If I called the cops, they would just assume it was me, and arrest me. And what if I tried to step in? All that would accomplish is me getting myself killed. No, it was best to just let someone else rescue this poor girl. It doesn't concern me, and I will be better off not getting involved. Eventually the screams went silent, and I though that would be the end of it. It wasn't.

The next day the police found her body in the alley. Broken, beaten, and bloody. No one came to help her. No one called 911. She screamed and screamed and I didn't lift a finger to do anything to save this young lady's life. Her blood was on my hands. How could I live with myself?

I eventually collected myself, and tried to live something of a normal life. Years passed and I had somehow managed to move on, and forget. My life was good, I was married to a beautiful woman, she was the love of my life. I had a decent job, it wasn't the greatest, but it paid the bills and I enjoyed what I did, and who I worked with. Everything seemed to be going right for me.

On a rather nondescript day, with nothing particularly noteworthy about it, I was out for a walk to get some fresh air, there was a hotdog stand, not too far from where I worked and I loved it. I had decided that I'd like to treat myself. While on my way I began thinking of my wonderful life and how happy I was to be alive. I thought about my wife, how our anniversary was just around the corner. I had no idea what I was going to get her. Flowers, and dinner of course, I had made reservations at the fanciest steak house in town. But I couldn't decide what gift I should buy her. Something to show her, just how much I really adore her. How much she means to me. I got completely lost in my own thoughts and I wasn't paying attention to where I was walking. I wasn't paying attention to the semi barreling down the street that I had just walked into. The horn blared snapping my mind back to reality, just in time for the impact.

When I first awoke I was in nothing. I believed it to be a hospital but quickly realized it was not. Everything was dark. It was like being in the stereotypical purgatory on TV, the all white empty space. Think of that, but with almost no light. And no light source either. The small amount of illumination in this place seemed to be coming out of nowhere. I lied there for several minutes trying to understand, trying to get my bearings, trying to remember what happened.

It all came flooding back, the day I was having, the morning at work, lunch time, my walk to get a hotdog, my getting lost in thought. The semi truck. I slowly rose to my feet decided it was best to walk around try to assess the situation. Once on my feet I knew immediately something was wrong. I felt no pain, given what had happened, I should be in excruciating pain, after all I did get hit by a semi, I should at least be bruised, and have a few bones broken. But I seemed to not have a scratch. That was impossible I had thought to myself, and it quickly dawned on me that I was dead.

I wasn't scared of dying as I had my faith and I knew that I was going to go to heaven. Slowly the little light that I had began to fade, and the nothingness began to fall away until I was back in the city. I didn't recognize this place, not at first. I stood there looking around struggling to figure out what was happening, and where I was.

The night seemed to be deathly quiet until a single scream pierced the silence and all at once I knew this is the girl from my past. That scream belonged to the young woman that I ignored all those years ago. I was back there. Except this time I wasn't up in my apartment trying not to hear the attack, trying not to here her begging for help. This time I was there. I was in the alley with her, behind me was a wall, I couldn't leave. I was forced to watch the brutal attack, four big men did unspeakable things to this poor girl. They stole her innocence. They beat her mercilessly, before ultimately ending her life. This is what I had ignored all those years ago, this is what I did nothing to prevent. This is what I allowed myself to forget about.

Seeing this with my own eyes was too much for me to

bare. I was in tears. I wept so hard that I didn't notice the city falling away, I didn't notice the darkness getting darker, I didn't notice the flames licking up around me, I didn't notice that all I could see through the blackness was this poor girl's attack. And then it started again. The whole attack ran it's course, only this time I could feel my skin boiling I could feel the agonizing emotional and physical pain. All I could do was cry. I was in Hell, it seems that I would live this moment over and over again for eternity. But then a hand breached the darkness and extended towards me. I grabbed it without giving it a second thought, I didn't care who was on the other end. It had to be better than were I was currently at. It pulled me back to the emptiness that I first woke up in.

The man was hooded and draped in a long flowing robe, it was beautiful, a material finer than silk. It was a darker black than the Hell that he rescued me from. I couldn't see his face, but the large frame that stood before me, forced the assumption that it was a man. He spoke. His words were soft, gentle, and sad. With every word he spoke I felt more comforting, he possessed the voice of an angel, I couldn't shake the feeling though, that the whole time, I was being deceived. That every word out of his mouth, was poison covered in sugar. Underneath his sweet and soothing tone there was something sinister in his voice. He explained that heaven needs more soldiers. He told me that Hell was becoming too populated. He told me about how Hell was becoming too powerful, he told me that there were too many people like me, good men who do nothing to stop evil, making us guilty. He told me that Heaven needed more souls. But the problem is that the only way to guarantee the soul will make it to Heaven. The only way to make sure that the person is pure enough, is to kill the body before it has a chance to taint the soul. To ensure Heaven gets the soul the body must be sacrificed while it is still an infant.

He told me that this is why I was rescued, I was given a second chance. I was a good person in life, who made one major mistake, and I was being given the opportunity to make things right. In exchange for life, in exchange of keeping me out of Hell. I have to make that sacrifice.

So here I am decades later. Watching the door, glancing at the clock, just waiting. Each year he comes, and each year we renew our contract. His arrival is always marked by the stopping of time, it's so cliche, I have to wonder if he does it for dramatic effect, or if it's just a side effect of a supernatural being crossing into this plane of existence. I continue to wait, suddenly my clocks stop, birds become frozen in mid air, he's here. To be a good host I stand up and walk to the door and open it. He's standing on the porch. I look at him for a second before turning around and heading back into the house without a word. He steps in behind me, almost gliding. I make a quip about the benefit's of time stopping that falls flat, he's not in a joking mood apparently.

I spin around and come face to face with him, well, face to shadow cast by his hood. He stares at my face, into my eyes, it feel like he's looking into my soul. "So down to business?" I scoff sourly, but he continues to stare. I look back at him, when he finally speaks, his response made my blood run cold.

"A bit of bad news about that soul, I'm afraid." He paused. "One, well one just isn't going to be enough anymore." He continued. To keep you here on Earth, we need more."

"You told me that Heaven only needs one!" I protest

shouting at him. "This isn't about Heaven it's about your own god damn greed..." I trailed off expecting denial, or some kind of explanation. Instead he just stood there seeming slightly amused at my outburst. I could feel his smile burning through the blackness of the shadow cast by his hood. It was hiding immense rage. I could feel that as well. But I was already rolling, and couldn't stop now. "You're no angel! You're a god damned greedy liar! You used me for your own gain! You tricked me into doing your bidding!" I paused, and turned away from him so as not to let him see how badly I was shaking. When I composed myself I turned around to continue my yelling but I did not get a chance to get out one word before he grabbed me by my collar and lifted me off of the ground.

"Now you will listen to me." it was stern, angry on the verge of shouting, the robe was cast off as two giant wings shot from his back, they were scorched and burned. Even so the spots of brilliant platinum shone through. The light dancing gloriously off the UN-scorched feathers. Yes his wings had been burnt and broken, but at one time they were beautiful, magnificent. The hatred and rage painted clearly across his face. Like his wings I could see that at one time his beauty was unmatched. His size was intimidating but the wings made him seem like a giant. I trembled before him silently begging for the mercy of this godlike being. He pulled me in very close, and began speaking again, his breath smelled of fire. "You knew I was lying from the start, and you still accepted." his voice calming down as his wings, and the rest of his body began to relax. "You're not innocent." He released my collar, and I took a step back to settle myself. "You knew what I was really offering and you chose to save yourself. Do not try to act self righteous." All I could do was glare at him in disgust, he was right.

Lucifer extends his hand, smiling once again.

"Deal?"

-THE HOUSE-

I'm scared, I'm terrified. I'm actually going to die in this house, I know that.

There is a house, every neighborhood, of every town. The haunted, run down, spooky house. The one that has been abandoned for decades, practically and in some cases full on condemned. The one that the neighborhood kids dare each other to go into. Well our neighborhood had one. And it was average as far as these things go.

This particular house carried stories of ghosts, ghouls, witches, the works. Like average, all the kids would dare each other to go in, none of them would. They would tell stories of disappearances, and murders. No one ever really disappeared though, it would have been big news in such a little town. Kids will be kids though, so the legends would continue to be passed.

Being a decent twenty something guy, I should have just ignored my more immature friends that would still pass the stories around. There's nothing really to say though, when my friends got to running their mouths, I had to get into to it with them. We would end up spending significant amounts of time arguing over this house. Was it really haunted? Was it evil? Were the stories we grew up on actually true? Of course they weren't, but it was fun to think they might be though.

The four of us had been friends for as long as I could remember. The town was small and our mothers had been great friends since before any of us were conceived, so it was kind of destined that we'd end up being a group. It was ok though, they were a good bunch of guys.

During one of our arguments we were at the local bar, we had all gotten a few drinks in us, and the house was brought up, I had a long day with a lot of stress, and a lot weighing on me. My future, my finances. So I wasn't in the mood and I shut it down. "The stories are just that, god damn stories," I paused looking at them. "Made up fiction." I snapped. They exchanged glances, I was normally the quieter one, I was level headed one in the group. I didn't have the strength to really protest, or go against the crowd like that. It's the reason that I was in the financial position that I was in, I couldn't find the balls to ask for a raise, and I couldn't quit, I was too much of a pushover for that too.

"Well," Rob said looking me up and down, he was much larger than me, and he was extremely intimidating if you didn't know him, fortunately I knew him well. And I knew he was a damn teddy bear so I shot his look right back at him.

"What." I spit back, very flatly.

"Well, if you're so convinced that it's all just legend, that there's nothing of about that house..." he trailed off and just looked at me, I knew where he was going with this and I started getting angry.

"What? You want me to spend the night?" My words came out sour. "What are you gonna dare me? Oh are you gonna triple dog dare me to?" I began looking at the others making it clear that I was addressing the whole group as I went on. "Get fucked! We're not children were grown ass men. It's about time we started acting the part." I sat there more angry at myself than them. Angry because of my situation, angry because I couldn't find this kind of courage to talk to my boss, angry that I was letting myself take it out on them.

Rob and the others exchanged looks, then he spoke.

"Yeah, Josh," he said my name very matter of factly like he didn't just witness my outburst. "Stay in the house, but not on a dare." He made air quotes, as he said dare. He was mocking me now. Before I had a chance to respond he started again. "On a bet…" The others began to snicker like they thought that idea was funny.

"Excuse me?" I was about to lose it again, he knew the troubles I was in, all three of them knew, they were my best friends, and they wanted to talk about betting!

"Look Josh, I know you're about to remind me of the meager paycheck you get, so don't lose the bet, eh?" I had to admit that he had a point. "You think it's all fake, none of it's real? Well I got a thousand dollars that says you're too much of a chicken shit to stay the night." Eddie and Mike quickly jumped in wanting a piece, both offering a thousand a piece. Three thousand dollars for staying one night in a supposedly haunted house. I could do it, I would love the money, I'm sure it was just a 'coincidence' that I happened to be just about three grand in debt. How I could I turn that down though?

"Sure Rob." I said I glanced at the other guys, gratitude oozing from my lips. "I'll uh, I'll go ahead and show you pansies there's nothing wrong with that house, and I'll take your money too. And when I do, I'll buy you all a round, with your own money." They laughed, I laughed and for the first time in a while I had a great time without crippling worry, in the back of my mind.

I would trade that worry for my current situation a thousand times over.

So Friday night rolled around, the day we were supposed to meet so I could go into the house. I stood outside the front gate, leaning against my car. We agreed to meet at eight, but being the person I am, I was there at seven thirty. Many thoughts ran through my head, could I really accept this much money from them? Would this change the dynamic of our relationship? I didn't suppose so, the reason that they chose this route was so that they're not 'giving' me any money, rather, I'm 'winning' it from them. I didn't know how to thank them for that. My thoughts continued to race. I would be in such a better place after this.

Eight o' clock, and they're not here, figures they'd all be late, my mind began to wander to the stories that surrounded the house, I even began to let myself wonder if they may have been true. For a second I began to have doubts but quickly scolded myself for being so, well, so stupid. About eight fifteen and here comes Mike cruising up, he stopped behind mine, and got out. "How's it going?" He asked walking around his car.

"Not too bad." He reached into his passenger window and grabbed something. "Gonna catch any demons tonight?" Jokingly questioning, I shook my head as he handed me a walkie. "They have thirty six hour battery life... I got three more so we can all stay connected," he paused and looked at me. "I-I also got you this." He extended his hand, I held out mine and he dropped it into my palm. A silver cross on a chain. I looked down at it for a moment. Then up to him, he was studying my face, and looked me in the eyes. "Ya know man, you don't have to go in there, ya know we could just give y-"

"No." I'm not a charity case, and I wasn't about to let him offer to hand me money he worked for. Before he could push the issue Rob and Eddie came pulling up. "Guess the decided to carpool." I said to Mike, nodding to the car. He kind of half smiled, nodded in agreement and mumbled something I couldn't make out, I'm sure that it was unimportant anyway. Something had him flustered, this worried me. Did he really believe in the legends? Was he actually scared of me going into the house? I tried to get a read on him, but my thoughts and the brief seconds of silence were interrupted when Rob and Eddie came over to us.

"Hey tough guy," Rob called out, in a mocking voice. "How is everyone going to spend their grand that were about to make huh?" I rolled my eyes, no one was really paying attention to him so his tone got a little more serious, kind of the way that Mike was acting. "Hey man, are-well are you sure you're going to be able to do this?" He paused looking me in the eyes.

"What the hell is the matter with you guys today? I'll be fine, it's just a house, I'm more in danger of falling through the loose floorboards than I am of something paranormal, or supernatural." The three men stood there looking at me, I shrugged. "So I brought some gear." I reached in my car and grabbed my bag. "Snacks, drinks, hammer, first aid, (for the aforementioned falling through the floor) gloves, rope, the basics."

"How about them nudie mags?" Eddie shot at me.

"No" I spit back and without missing a beat. "I got pictures of your wife on my phone, that should do the trick tonight." It got a decent laugh from the group, and it made me smile. "Oh I almost forgot, I did bring a blanket, and a pillow, with any luck I'll catch a few Zs while I'm in there."

I grabbed my stuff, and Mike passed out the walkies, I took a deep breath and headed into the house, I was halfway up the walk, when I realized I didn't have my pillow, and blanket. I turned my head and asked one of the guys to grab it. Eddie scooped up the little bundle I had made, and jogged over while I continued walking. I was just inside the house looking around when Eddie called out to me. He was standing at the edge of the porch. "What Eddie? Can you bring me my stuff please?" He continued to stand there, finally shaking his head no. I think he was ashamed to admit that this place terrified him. Slightly disgusted, I let out a deep sigh. "Fine." I said in a sarcastically sympathetic tone. "I'll come grab my stu-" I was cut off. I fell down, as if knocked to the ground. "Eddie help me! Please! Something's got me!" The terror that washed over his face was indescribable, he quickly gained his bearings and charged for the door.

Eddie stood over me, in a panic, while I could no longer contain myself. I burst out in a fit of hysterical uncontrollable laughter! When I began to be able to breathe again, I extended a hand for him to help me up. He did, reluctantly. "Oh my god, I got you so good." He just stared at me. "You should have seen the look on your face! I so wish that I was recording that! It would have gone viral!" Eddie just turned around stepped out of the house, down the steps, and onto the walk way. He stopped there, turned around and looked me in the eyes and said very flat and emotionless

"Good luck." It sent a shiver down my spine. I watched him get back to the others, they fanned out a bit, so we could test the walkie talkies, they worked. It was time to get this night started.

The first thing that I did, was pull out my phone, one of the terms of the deal was that I needed to do short video recordings every hour or so, to prove that I'm still here. I started the recording and went on a tour of the house, it had three bedrooms, two bathrooms, the rooms were on the second floor, I'm sure at one point this house was beautiful, it had a living room, and a family room, a kitchen of decent size and a large dining room, this was definitely a house made for a big family. The furniture that was left behind was ancient and falling apart. It was probably infested too, so I decided that the floor would be the best place to lie down, I set up a little spot for myself in the living room, picked up the walkie talkie, and began chatting up the guys outside.

Everything was quiet for a good long while, I watched a couple videos on my phone. I soon grew sleepy though, and so I set an alarm for ninety minutes out, let the group know I was going to pass out for a little bit, and I laid down and fell asleep. I awoke to a loud crash upstairs. It sounded like a bookshelf toppled over. I remembered seeing one in one of the rooms at the far end of the hall, so (like an idiot) I headed up to investigate. To be perfectly honest, I figured the shelf was old, the books while deteriorating would still have to be heavy. I stopped suddenly at the bottom of the steps as I heard something that made my blood run cold. Footsteps. Coming from the same area as the first crash. It only took me a few heartbeats to come to the conclusion that one of my stupid ass friends are in the room. He climbed through the window, fell in, and is now walking around.

As I got closer to the room, I could clearly here him walking around, and he was talking to someone, I couldn't hear what he was saying, but he definitely sounded angry. I figure he was talking into the walkie on a different channel, so I stood outside the door, clicking through channels. I should have just gotten the hell out of there, when I couldn't find anything on any of the channels on the walkie. I didn't. I began listening again, I could hear the voice again, and the footsteps. With one swift movement, I took a step grabbed the door handle, swung the door wide open and burst into... an empty room. The bookshelf still in place.

I couldn't do anything but stand there, I couldn't move,

I could barely think. After a few long minutes I pulled the walkie off my hip with a shaking hand, and spoke into it "Are- are you guys still out there?" I got three confirmations. I began moving through the mostly empty room. I became more terrified, this wasn't a bedroom, it was an office. No windows. The bookshelf was bolted to the wall, the desk while falling apart remained upright. I couldn't explain what I heard with any rational reasoning other than auditory hallucinations. I was lying to myself, but it was a comforting lie, so I allowed myself to believe it, and headed back down the living room where I had set up my little camp.

My mind continued to race, I wanted to leave so bad, I thought hard about it. I knew my friends wouldn't hold me to the bet. But I also knew I needed that money. Bad. So I decided to stick it out. The silence that filled the room was that loud painful silence. Almost deafening, only rivaled by the intense sound of my heart beating ready to burst from my chest, louder it got, and harder it was beating, I felt as if I was going to die right there. Panic began to wash over me, my lungs began to burn, and all at once my senses returned. I opened my mouth and took a huge deep breath, then slowly let it out. I got so caught up in the nothing that I had unintentionally stopped breathing.

I was in desperate need of a distraction, so I grabbed the walkie. "Is anyone there?" I spoke soft and timidly.

"..." Nothing on the other end.
"Come on guys, someone say something."
"..."
"This isn't funny ass holes you're supposed to be out there waiting for me" I was getting frustrated at this point, why weren't they answering me?

"..."

I tossed the walkie aside, and started mumbling, I assumed they had fallen asleep, it was a short amount of time since I last talked to them, but I also assumed they have been drinking. I guess it's true what they say about making assumptions though.

With no one on the other line to talk to me, I shot another little update video, and explained what happened in the room, then cursed at the guys for falling asleep on me. I then decided to watch a little YouTube at this point, as sleeping for me was one hundred percent out the window. Things went smoothly, I watched a few cat video, and some gaming videos, I even watched a creepy pasta video or two. (probably not my smartest idea.) They started getting my nerves up and running again, so I turned them off, I just shut off the screen and sat in the darkness for a while. I had been putting too much strain on my phone as it began to die.

Fifteen percent the phone rung out with the notification.

It startled me, shattering the silence, and I almost leapt out of my own skin. At the same time though, I thought I heard someone laugh, a little girl, it was faint but it came from the kitchen. There was a very small narrow hallway leading to the kitchen. I peered down it, but didn't see anything. I tried to forget it, I didn't hear anything, it was my phone echoing through this empty rundown house. But then I heard it again, clear as day. I spun to gaze down the hallway just as my eyes land on the darkness I saw something. It was just a shadow, and moved quickly into the kitchen out of my line of sight. I rushed after it, whoever it was, she was short and had the laugh of a young girl. What the hell was she doing in here, she could get seriously hurt. I burst into the kitchen but it was empty, the dining room was empty. I slowly searched that side of the house, but it was all empty. No way she got back by me without noticing. I walked very hesitantly back towards the living room, I was about halfway down the hall, when I heard the voice again. The voice, this time, called from living room. it wasn't laughter this time though. "Don't be mad, I was just getting a glass of water." She sounded scared. I was frozen in place. I rushed into the living room, just as I heard her footsteps round the top of the stairs. I should have been scared, but something took over, I guess it was protector instincts because all I could think of was I need to find this young girl, and keep her safe. I made it to the top of the steps and stared down the hall. She was gone, she must have ducked into one of the rooms. Again my instincts wouldn't allow me to think clearly, I started moving towards the first bedroom. Then I heard it. A blood curdling scream from the far room! I ran, when I got there I pushed the door. The knob wouldn't turn the door wouldn't open. I yelled to stand back and sent the door flying into the room with a hard swift kick. I stood there panting, shaking, the adrenaline coursing through my veins. I looked around, the room was empty.

I couldn't believe it. I couldn't fucking believe it... here I was, once again, in an empty room, where I know I heard someone. This time a young girl, in the office an angry man. I think I was starting to piece together what was going on in this house. Once again, I had to scold myself. I was nervous before coming in here, and the horror narrations just made my nerves worse. I sat down in the middle of the room and really just looked around as I let my mind wander. I could see that this was definitely a little girls room, the walls now faded and cracked seem to have been a bright shade of pink at one time, the rug on the wooden floor seemed whimsical.

I took a deep breath and willed myself to my feet. Was completely at a loss. I literally had no idea what to do, should I leave the house? I stumbled around, and into the hallway. The next thing I did was move to the next room. I could see this was a boys room, I was in here earlier on my tour, but I hadn't really been looking though it. I noticed a rotted out bed, a few little trucks, other such trinkets in the room. I stood there, just taking it all in. There was nothing really out of the ordinary in this room. I walked out and down the hall, I stopped outside the office, the door still slightly open from earlier. I just waited but heard nothing, after a few seconds I got my nerve up and peaked into the room, it was still empty. I made my way down the hallway and stopped outside the last door. I pressed my ear against the door, but I didn't hear anything. I got down on all fours and peeked under the door, and saw nothing. I opened the door, and walked around the room.

I didn't know what I was doing, what I expected to gain from memorizing the rooms, but after what I had experienced I really didn't know what else to do. Everything was quiet and calm again. I started back toward the steps, half way down I got my phone out to make another recording. I detailed the little girl screaming, and then disappearing. The only thing I could think of is that I was tired, and scared. I didn't include the narrative that my brain was working on. There was a story unfolding but I didn't allow myself to believe it. I needed some sleep. I went back to my indoor camp site, put on some happier music to take my mind off everything and laid my head down for some rest.

I closed my eyes and they shot back open as soon as I did. I heard stomping, on the children's side of the house upstairs, I squeezed my eyes shut and tried to cover my ears. I didn't want to hear whatever it was that was going on. I heard the door rattle as if locked, then something hit it. I heard something hit the door over and over, I heard the wood splinter and crack. For a minute it all went silent, then I heard a little boy scream! And with that once again my instincts took over and I dashed for the stairs. I tore up them around the corner, and down the hall. The door sat open. I had heard it crack. When I went into the room... I was almost knocked off of my feet by the smell, the warm irony smell. The blood was everywhere. It looked as if someone was hacked up with an ax Then I seen the boy, his lifeless body laying broken, and bloody. As I mentioned before, I am a timid man, and this was too much. The world faded to black as my eyes rolled back in my head.

I sat up on the floor, it took just a second to remember what was going on. I frantically scanned the room, but miraculously, all the blood, and the body was gone. I was sitting in the middle of an empty room. That was it. I had had enough. I started making my way towards the stairs, the go was a little slow on my shaky legs. I stopped and grabbed my walkie. I squeezed the button and screamed into it. "i don't care about the money! I don't care about the god damn bet! I'm getting my ass out of this house!" And with that I started off again, I made it to the steps and began taking them one by one watching my feet land on each step. Half way down I heard the voice of a woman.

"I'm so sorry." I looked up, expecting not to see anything, but there she was a younger woman, late twenties, early thirties.

"It's too late for sorry." I heard a rough man's voice, angry and full of hate coming from behind me. "i cant go back from this point!" I spun around and at the top of the steps, there stood a big intimidating man, he was panting, covered in blood. He was holding an ax

"You-you didn't?!" The woman screamed. The man smiled a sadistic smile and lunged forward at her... at me. I attempted to defend myself, to block him, but he seemed to pass right through me. He buried his ax into the woman's face, and her body went limp. He ripped it from her face, swung it over her head, and hit her body again. He hit it again and again, over and over. I got by him and went for the door. a few steps away from safety I felt him grab my arm. I yanked hard but his grip was like a vice. Then I heard him speak to me

"Don't worry pal, it'll be ok, it has to be done." I thought he was going to kill me right now. I jerked and struggled and managed to get free I made it to the door and ripped it open. I quickly charged through, catching my foot on the bottom of the frame and fell flat on my face. I got up quickly as the door slammed behind me.

"No...no...no! No! No! This cannot be happening!" I didn't even realize that I was screaming. I was so shocked and terrified to see that when I stood up... I was still in the living room. how could that be? I ran out the door! How could I still be in the house? I grabbed at the knob and twisted. The door didn't open. I pulled harder and the knob came off in my hand. I hit the door with my shoulder but it wouldn't budge

I ran to the back door, the knob was gone! I hit the door and it likewise wouldn't budge. In a panic I ran to the window and kicked it, I expected to fall right through, but to my surprise I just bounced off of it. I kicked it and kicked it, it was like I was kicking solid concrete! I sat down and lost it. I bawled my eyes out for a good long while before my mind snapped to the ax man. He seemed to be gone, I was alone. I stood up, and found my walkie talkie. I screamed into it. I begged for anyone to help me. I begged them to come get me out! A weak voice cracked through the speaker. "I'm so sorry." I didn't understand! Feeling terrified, confused and angry I began trying to bust down the door again. I hit it until, I was physically drained. I fell to the ground and passed out.

When I awoke I was still here... and I repeated the same cycle. I hit the door over and over until I had no energy left, and collapsed. And that brings us to the beginning. There's no way for me to get out of this house... I know, I know this is where I'll die. Until then, I will continue to try to break down this door!

"We shouldn't have made that bet." Rob said looking at Eddie and Mike. "We should have just given him the money, we shouldn't have forced him into that house."

"No!" Mike snapped. "I tried to ask him not to go, I tried to tell him that we could just give him the money... he made his own decision."

The three men walked up to the doctor, "So, how is he?" Rob asked, mustering what little false hope he could The doctor was a little flustered.

"He's very delusional... I'm afraid were going to have to restrain him, he just keeps..." The doctor stopped mid sentence. The three men waited not so patiently for the doctor to continue. "He just keeps saying that he needs to get out of the house. and he keeps slamming into the door of his cell, as if trying to break it down."

-TWO SENTENCE STORIES-

"Never have I ever killed anyone." All eyes fell upon me, as the five men before me raised their bottles to their lips and began to drink.

I awoke, unable to move due to sleep paralysis. I began to panic when I heard dirt being shoveled onto the top of the coffin.

I stood outside those pearly gates as the archangel read in his book. He looked me in the eyes and said; "your sins will not be forgiven."

It's hard for me to accept, but I have to. I'm not human anymore.

The celebration over the first successful time machine turned to horror as the new announcement was broadcast. "be with your loved ones tonight, there is no tomorrow."

Watching a passenger jet take off is a breath taking experience. It's a shame it'll never reach it's destination. My brother waved at me from a passing bus.

He rode the bus everywhere, in fact he died on a bus when it wrecked last year.

When they exhumed the body, they were shocked to find scratch marks on the inside of the lid. They were even more shocked when his lifeless corpse sunk it's teeth into her neck.

-THANK YOU-

Aaron Forman for Cover Art
Metalfaceproductions@gmail.com
Faith Oswald for the illustrations
Faithnoswald@gmail.com

FOR ALL THE KICKSTARTER BACKERS THAT MADE THIS BOOK POSSIBLE.

AND A SPECIAL THANKS TO
Wolfie Chick
Sergeant Riegel
Michalene Crockett

www.ingramcontent.com/pod-product-compliance
Lightning Source LLC
Chambersburg PA
CBHW071133200626
46817CB00018B/2931